This book belongs to:

_____

♥

Daring Journey

JENNA LEE

Life as a teenager is difficult even under the best circumstances. Academic stress, social anxiety, and peer pressure are tough enough, but sometimes those challenges can be so overwhelming that they lead to self-destructive behaviour that can snowball until it can be hard to see a way out of all this heartache. Daring Journey is a collection of short stories written specifically for this time in your life. Each story ends with a love letter to your teenage self from someone who's endured similar difficulties.

Join Jenna Lee as she guides you down the path of self-discovery while offering tips and advice on how to overcome your challenges. And most of all, the understanding that you're not alone. If you're ready to embrace your unique self, Daring Journey will show you the way.

Trigger warning: Daring Journey does cover some heavy topics that may cause trigger warnings if you are or have gone through something similar. It's recommended for ages 16+.

Note: The information in Daring Journey is not intended as a substitute for the medical advice of physicians. The reader should regularly consult a physician in matters relating to his/her health and particularly with respect to any symptoms that may require diagnosis or medical attention. The information in Daring Journey is based on own experiences and fictional characters and is no way medical or psychological advice.

Copyright © 2019 Jenna Lee
All rights reserved.

First published in Australia 2019 by Daring Journey.

The right of Jenna Lee to be identified as the author of this work has been asserted by her under the *Copyright Amendment (Moral Rights) Act 2000*.

This work is copyright. Apart from any use as permitted under the *Copyright Act 1968*, no part of this publication may be reproduced, stored in a retrieval system, recorded or transmitted in any form or by any means, electronic, mechanical, photocopying, recording or otherwise, without the prior written permission of the publisher.

This is a work of fiction. Names, characters, businesses, places, events, locales, and incidents are either the products of the author's imagination or used in a fictitious manner. Any resemblance to actual persons, living or dead, or actual events is purely coincidental.

Formatting and interior design: KILA Designs www.kiladesigns.com.au
Editor: Lauren Clarke Editing www.creatingink.com/
Cover Design: Denise Krekling

Contents

Wearing A Mask   1

Friendship check-in
Things in common check-in
Drinking check-in
Love Letter to my teenage self

I'm Not Beautiful Like You   33

Comparison check-in
Self-love check-in
Love Letter to my teenage self

I Can't Do This Anymore   59

Self-care check-in
Reaching out check-in
Reaching Out check-in 2.0
Love Letter to my teenage self

Use Your Voice   81

Confidence check-in
Love Letter to my teenage self

Contents

The Inner Critic — 107
Inner Critic Check-In
Journal writing check-in
Love Letter to my teenage self

Can't You Understand — 129
Discrimination check-in
Love Letter to my teenage self

Think Before You Type — 143
Suicide check-in
Love Letter to my teenage self

Trust Issues — 163
Trust check-in
Save & Love yourself first
Love Letter to my teenage self

Contents

Embrace Our Differences — 185

Be You check-in
Own It check-in
Drop The Mask, Darling
Love Letter to my teenage self

Picture Perfect Vs Reality — 211

Morning routine check-in
Meditation
The Real You check-in
Social Media check-in
Love Letter to my teenage self

Stand Up — 229

Use Your Voice check-in
Love Letter to my teenage self

Blame Game — 241

Blame Game check-in
Love Letter to my teenage self

Contents

Teenage Boys — 251

Body Image
Peer pressure / Putting on a mask
Suicide
Depression

About The Author — 259
Keep the Daring Journey going — 260
Daring Support — 261
Recommended Resources — 262
Thank You — 263
Daring Journal — 264

Dear reader,

I see you sitting there, **alone** in your room. I see the **hurt** lining your face, and the defeat shrouding your shoulders. You don't think anyone understands. But **I see you.**

You're gripping my book and wondering **why** it was on your bed. You're **angry** with your parents for giving it to you, angry at the book, and just plain angry; you throw it across the room. But it doesn't really make you **feel better**, and the book keeps staring at you. So, you pick it up and turn it over to read the synopsis. In two paragraphs, you feel the first stirrings of **hope**. Maybe I'm not alone. Maybe someone else understands my pain. Maybe this book will give me a new **perspective** and help me manage my anxiety. For the first time in far too long, there is **light** at the end of this dark and lonely tunnel.

I know you're ready for this. I'm here, I'm with you, and we are in this together.

May Daring Journey guide you and be there for you when you need it the most.

With **love**,

Jenna Lee x

Daring
Adjective

To have the courage

to be fearless.

Journey

Noun

Movement from one stage of life to another.

Good friends pick you up when you've fallen.

Wearing a Mask

The doorbell rings. My heart hammers against my chest. I take a deep breath and make my way there. I reach the door and look to the mirror. I fix my top, brushing down the creases. *Here goes nothing.*

Candace pushes her way through the door. Lee, Kelley, and Rose follow close behind. I step back, letting everyone inside.

"Hey girls," I say as I shut the door behind them.

"God, I'm so keen for tonight, girl," Candace says, flicking her hair behind her shoulder.

"Me too." I smile, leading them to my bedroom.

I haven't had anyone over to my place for a while. I've always preferred going to my friends' places. It's easier. When my friends come here, they just want to hang out with my older brother and his friends who are always around. And then I find myself alone in my room.

The girls put their bags on the floor. Lee and Kelley sit on my bed. They start pulling out clothes, trying to find something to wear. Candace walks around my room, checking everything out. I quickly glance over, double-checking I put everything away. Photos of me and my family. My diaries and other stupid things. I want Candace to think that I'm cool, not a loser.

"You have to wear that halter dress, Lee. It looks perfect on you with your build," Candace says, looking Lee up and down.

Lee nods, pulling out the black halter from her bag before she unzips her school dress and gets undressed.

I scratch at my arms nervously. *What will she think of what I picked out to wear? Will it be up to her standards?*

"What are you wearing, Sophie?" Candace asks, moving towards her bag.

My heart starts to beat faster. I move to my closet and pull out the light blue denim singlet dress. I show the girls. Lee and Kelley don't say anything, just look to Candace.

"It's cute, I suppose," she says, reaching into her bag.

My cheeks turn red. I knew it wouldn't be good enough. But it's all I have to wear.

Candace pulls something out of her bag: two six-packs of premixed vodka and soda.

"Let's start drinking. We want to get tipsy before the show." Candace smirks, handing the girls their drinks. She passes me one and I hesitate.

"I've never had one before," I admit, unable to make eye contact.

The girls start laughing.

"Oh my God. Are you serious?" Candace says, covering her mouth.

I nod, leaning back against my cupboard. I've seen people drinking but I've never wanted to myself. But if they are drinking and think it's cool, I have to. Don't I?

"Come on, you have to have one. You will love it; trust me," Candace says, handing me a drink.

I grab it and screw off the top. The girls are all watching me, waiting. Bringing it to my lips, I tip it back, letting the liquid down my throat. It tastes so good. Just like a soft drink, only better. I grin before drinking more.

"See? Knew you would love it. Now let's get ready and down all these before we have to go."

After two drinks, I feel a buzz. Like I could take on the world. My head feels lighter. It's amazing. I get dressed in front of the girls, not caring if they see me in my ugly polka-dot underwear. The drinks give me the confidence to just be who I want to be. Who I really am. I haven't stopped smiling.

Looking myself over in the mirror, I feel great. The girls help by doing my hair, putting it up into a cute high ponytail. I apply some lipstick and am

ready to go. I feel like dancing.

"Come on, let's get going. It's time to par-tay," I say, then giggle.

"I love drunk Sophie—she's a laugh," Candace says, and the other girls nod in agreement.

Yes, they like me. This is going great—better than I could have ever imagined.

The Uber shows up about thirty minutes later. I can't remember who arranged it. I finish off my fourth or maybe fifth drink.

Lee hooks her arm through mine and we walk out the front of my house. The cool air hits my face and I close my eyes. I can't wait to get to the show. I just hope my brother, Brendan, doesn't let me down. The tickets should be at the door. He promised.

The Uber is parked out the front and we all get inside. About thirty minutes later, we are pulling up to the bar. The door opens and I step out. I lose my balance and trip over, landing on my hands and knees. The girls laugh but don't help me. My head spins and I take a moment to clear it enough to get back up. I sway but manage to catch up with the girls who are talking to the guards on the bar door. I stop in the middle of the footpath and take in the crowd. There's a huge line that goes all the way down the street. Everyone's talking loudly and cheering.

"Sophie, come here. This guy wants to see you," Candace yells over the noise.

I join the girls before telling him that Brendan has tickets for us on hold. He nods and disappears inside.

"You better hope that your brother pulls through, Sophie," Candace says.

I ignore her, staring at the door the guy went through. *Please, I need this to go smoothly.*

I hope my brother did as he promised. Or this will be it for me. Back to being a nobody.

The bouncer appears and waves us through. He doesn't even ask us for our IDs. I follow behind Candace and into the darkness of the club.

Time passes in a blur and I find myself at the bar with shots lined up in front of me. They are all empty and my head is killing.

Loud knocking wakes me from a deep sleep. I sit in my bed and instantly regret it. My head is thumping. I run my hand through my hair and hiss through my teeth. Pain travels through my arm. I look down and gasp. My face feels numb. The door to my bedroom flies open, and my brother storms in. I catch his eye and wish I hadn't. He looks furious; he can't even maintain eye contact with me. My chest tightens. What have I done?

"Mum and Dad will be back in a few minutes. Clean up the shit show out here."

The door slams shut. It takes me a moment to try to get myself together. What the hell happened last night? The last thing I remember is getting into the bar for my brother's show. The rest is a complete blur. There's gravel rash running from my wrist down to my elbow. I push back my sheets. There are more grazes on both of my legs, mainly on my knees. I must have fallen last night and hurt myself. I bring my knees against my chest and rock back and forth, taking deep breaths.

"Sophie!" my brother yells.

I slowly rise to a standing position. The room starts to spin. Blackness tries to consume me. It takes me a moment before everything comes back into focus. After grabbing some pants out of my cupboard, I put them on.

My brother wasn't kidding; it's a complete mess out here. There are bottles all around the kitchen bench and on the table. Did I bring people back? I don't have time to think about it as I clean the kitchen in record time. Just as I put the last bottle in the bin, I hear the garage door opening. I'm not ready to face my parents just yet. I run into the bathroom and turn on the shower.

Removing my clothes takes a lot longer than normal as I try not to touch my sores. Once undressed, I look at myself in the mirror. I take a step back and let out a gasp before stepping closer to the mirror. There's gravel rash down one side of my face, from the corner of my eye down to the side of my

lip. It looks nasty. I can't breathe.

I don't recognise the girl in the mirror. She's got black rings around her eyes. Her pupils are dilated, and she has nasty gravel marks all over her body. Her hair is a complete mess, full of knots that will take a week to get out. I turn away, unable to look at her for another second.

The hot water burns my skin, but I don't move. I like the way it stings my skin. I lean back against the shower wall. My arms cling around my tummy. It's getting hot in here. My head starts to become blurry. I fall down to the tiles, landing on my hands and knees. The water streams all around me. My chest tightens and I feel hotter and hotter. I clench my tummy as I expel everything I can. Nothing comes out apart from red liquid.

Once everything's come up, I lean back against the shower screen. There's a knock on the bathroom door and my heart beats faster. *Please, please don't come in.* I need to get my shit together before facing my parents.

"Sophie, we need to talk. Now." My father's voice sends a shiver down my spine.

Shit, they know. Chills run through my body and I try not to dry-retch.

"I'm coming," I yell back.

I spend another few minutes in the shower trying to drag out the time. After turning off the water, I step out of the shower and cover myself with a towel. I put on my dressing gown. I need to cover myself up. I don't want my parents seeing any more of my sores.

I take one last look at myself in the mirror. My scabs are covered, well, apart from the one on my face, I still feel like complete shit. The black bags under my eyes haven't changed. My brown hair is slicked back away from my face, water dripping all around me. I move away before I find any more faults.

Turning the doorknob, I take several deep breaths. My dad comes around the corner; he takes one look at me and his eyes widen.

"Meet me in the living room," he snaps.

He turns away and my heart shatters. I'm in deep shit. I dry off my hair with my towel as best I can and throw it into the laundry on my way past. I cling to my dressing gown, drawing it tighter around my body as a protection against what's to come. I walk slowly down the hallway, counting down. Five, four, three, two, one. My legs shake as I take the final step around the corner.

My parents are sitting on the couch on the far side of the room. I sit opposite them, next to Brendan who's on his phone. I look to my mother and she lets out a cry and covers her mouth with her hand.

"Want to explain to us what happened last night? Why you had friends over here drinking and you went out to a bar?" My father's voice gets louder with each word.

I glare straight at Brendan before raising my brows. How could he rat me out to our parents? I thought we had a deal.

He drops his phone and puts his hands up in surrender. "It wasn't me. You missed a drink can in your bedroom. They found it and drilled me for answers," Brendan explains, shrugging like it's not a big deal. My parents will never permit me to leave this house again. I catch my mother's eye, she's stayed silent. She shakes her head.

"I don't know what you want me to say. But I guess I'm sorry." I shrug.

I'm not sorry for drinking and going out with my friends. They don't understand that it's everything to hang with those girls. For once in my life, I had a chance to be in with them and I would do it again in a heartbeat. I do feel bad for going behind my parents' back but it's what I had to do.

"You guess?" my father growls.

"I just wanted to spend time with my new friends."

"Ones who encourage you to go behind your parents' backs, drink, and use you to get tickets to your brother's show? They don't sound like friends who I would want to hang out with," my mother pipes up. "And what happened to your face?"

I let out a sigh and cover my face with my hands. Pain explodes through me and I pull back.

"You disappointed us, Sophie. We can't trust you to stay here with your brother over the next week while we are away in Queensland. We will be dropping you off at your grandparents'," my father says and walks away without a backwards glance.

"But I have school?" I protest.

"Think of it as a holiday. The decision is final, and maybe a week away with your grandparents will help you. I don't know what's gotten into you. This lying and going behind our backs? It isn't you, Sophie," my mother says with a sigh.

She walks off into the kitchen, leaving me with my brother.

"Mum's right, Sophie. Those girls aren't who you should be hanging around with. They are bad news. They hang off older guys and they left you in a bad way last night. They don't care about you."

"But I need them to like me, Brendan. I have to fit in with the cool kids. I'm a nobody and I need to be a somebody." I huff.

Brendan shakes his head and leaves me on the couch by myself.

I understand where my family is coming from, but I need to be a part of that group. What did he mean about them leaving me in a bad way last night? I can't remember a thing; the whole night is a complete blackout. I'm sure they wouldn't have left me in a harmful situation. I woke up in my own bed so they must have helped me get home. Didn't they?

I shake off my thoughts and get ready to go to my grandparents' place. I'll have enough time over the next week to put the pieces together of what happened last night.

We pull up to my grandparents' place three hours later. My nan is waiting on the front porch for us. She smiles and waves to us as we drive down her steep driveway. As soon as Dad turns the car off, Nan opens my door. I step out and she pulls me in for a hug. I instantly relax in her arms, inhaling her signature smell of roses. She kisses me on the head and pulls away.

"Where's Pop?" I ask as he would normally be out to greet us. I catch a worried look in my nan's eye but it's gone before I can question it.

"Oh, he's just inside watching the football. He'll catch us soon."

She takes my bags off my parents and I walk down to the lemon trees at the back of the house, giving them time to talk. The birds are singing; it's such a beautiful day. *Too bad I feel like shit.* My head is still thumping, and I haven't been able to keep anything down. I guess this is what a hangover feels like. Like death.

"Come back up here. Your pop will be dying to see you," Nan yells.

I say my goodbyes to my parents, and they kiss me. As soon as they drive off, Nan takes my hand and we head inside. She doesn't say a word about what happened, even though I know my parents would have just filled her in. That's the thing I love most about my nan—she never judges me. She just gives me advice on how to learn from my mistakes. She reassures me that we all stuff up and it's how we learn from it that matters most.

Their house is an old white weatherboard that's divided into two separate dwellings. There is a little one-bedroom unit at the back that they use for visitors. Their house is right in front and it's got two bedrooms. It's pretty tight but it works for them. My father grew up here with his brothers.

Nan puts my bags in the front room. I head past the kitchen into the living room where I find my pop in his recliner, watching the footy. He's yelling at the TV with a beer in his hand. I've never seen him without a beer, no matter what time of day.

"Hey, Pops," I say before kissing him on his cheek.

"Hey, sweetie. I hear that you've been getting up to some mischief." He coughs and it doesn't sound good at all.

"You okay?"

"Oh, he's fine, darling. Just a cough," Nan says dismissively. If Nan thinks it's nothing, it must be that.

She brings in some lemon slice and a cup of green tea for me. She knows that I love her famous slice. It's to die for but I honestly don't know if I can keep it down today. She must catch my scrunched-up nose.

"Just take little bites; you need something in that tummy of yours." I smile. *God, I love her.*

I spend the rest of the afternoon watching the footy with Pop while Nan heads down the street to get something for dinner. No doubt we will be having meat and three veg.

Lying back on the couch, I go to reach for my phone, then I remember that I don't have it. My mother took it with them, saying that it will do me some good to be without it for the next week. *What the hell am I meant to do?* I need it to find out what the hell happened last night. My friends are most likely trying to message and call me to make sure I'm okay. I let out a huff, throwing my hand down against the couch.

"What's got your knickers in a knot?" Pop asks.

"I don't have my phone. I need it to talk to my friends and find out what happened last night," I say honestly. Pop's like Nan; I can be totally honest with him too.

"Pfft, it's not the end of the world. You kids spend too much time on those bloody things. The break will do you some good. Besides, you will find out when you go back in a week. Suck it up, princess."

I laugh. He's right. It will be fine. I just have to get through the week. Nan and Pop are old school and don't have a computer or laptop so there's no sneaking to get on.

After dinner, I take another shower. I'm feeling much better now that I have something in my stomach. I wrap my towel around me and walk to my room. I pass Nan on my way through the kitchen. She gasps and I instantly stop. Her eyes are wide open.

"What?" I ask, raising my brows.

"Oh my God, look at those sores. They are terrible. Here, I'll get some ointment that will help heal them. What happened?"

"I wish I knew, Nan, but I have no idea. I woke up and the night was a complete blackout."

"It will be okay. Go dress and we will get these fixed up."

I nod and walk off to my bedroom. Shutting the door behind me, I look down at my sores. *Shit. She's right; they are bad.* I saw them earlier today but didn't really have a good look. The gravel rash that travels down both my arms is angry and raw. My knees are torn apart, with bruises coming through under the grazes. And then there's my face—I must have fallen straight on it.

Shaking my head, I slowly get dressed, trying not to brush against them. I sit on my bed and place my face in my hands. I wish I knew what happened. *What have I done?*

Nan comes in and she offers me a smile as she applies the ointment. I hiss through my teeth as she puts it on my face and then my knees. She hits one tender spot and I reach out, grabbing her arm.

"Just sit still. This is going to help in the long run."

"I hope you're right, Nan."

After she's finished, she tucks me into bed and kisses me good night. "We all make mistakes, sweetheart. Just know that our family doesn't have a good track record with drinking, so don't tempt fate, Sophie."

She switches off the light and I think over what she said. I know my pop drinks a lot, but I didn't think it was an issue? Maybe there is more to it.

I lie in bed wide awake, playing every scenario of what could have happened last night in my head. *What will occur when I go back to school next week? Will everything be back to normal?* I have to hold on to the hope that it will be.

I spend the next week helping Nan and Pop clean out the unit at the back of their house. They help me keep my mind off thinking about things but at night, it is the worst.

I'm back at home in my bedroom unpacking my bag. Someone knocks on my door.

"Come in."

I turn to see my mother. She's carrying something behind her back. I look at her in question.

"I'm glad your sores have healed and that you're feeling better." She smiles. "I would like to keep this for another week, but I think being away at your grandparents', you've had some time to think about what happened. Have you learnt your lesson?"

"I'm sorry for lying to you both and going behind your back," I say, knowing that's exactly what she wants to hear. I need to get my phone back to reply to

my friends. They probably think that I'm dead.

My mother smiles and passes me my lifeline. I wrap my arms around her, giving her a tight squeeze. She leaves and I jump onto my bed with my phone in my hands.

I turn it on and pause. My stomach starts to churn as I wait for it to light up. My breathing picks up as it switches to life. A full minute passes, but nothing comes up.

Something's got to be wrong with this. It should be full of messages. Shouldn't it?

I open my texts again and my Facebook messenger, there's still nothing apart from a message from Ashley seeing if I'm okay. I haven't talked to her since she ditched me at a party a few weeks ago. But what about my new friends? What about Candace? *Why didn't she message me?*

I start rocking back and forth on my bed. *What have I done?*

We pull up to school early. My father stops but I don't get out. I hold on to my stomach. I think I'm going to be sick.

"Come on, Sophie. I need to get to work."

"Give me a second," I say through gritted teeth.

I reach for the door handle and my hands start to shake. *Let's go, Sophie, everything's going to be fine.* But why didn't one of the girls message me?

Opening my door, the wind flicks my hair back away from my face. After I shut the door, my father drives off and I stand there on the side of the road, watching his car disappear.

I take a deep breath and start putting one foot in front of the other until I'm finally at my locker. I place my books inside and lean against the cool surface. I'm here early, so I look down at my phone. Flicking through Facebook while I wait, I'm again reminded that my friends didn't check up on me. I desperately need answers as to why. There is probably an explanation and once I hear it, everything will go back to normal.

Time passes and every time I hear the door open, I check but it's not my friends.

Finally, I glance over to find Candace and Lee, Kelley, Rose, and *what the ... Ashley? Since when does she hang with them?*

They are walking down the corridor. When they get closer, I wave. My heart starts racing faster and faster. None of them smile back. *Why aren't they smiling at me?*

Candace looks me up and down, then she walks straight past me. My bottom lip starts to tremble but I try to hide it. Maybe she didn't see me, but I know she did.

A group of girls from the year below walk by and stop in front of me. A girl with curly red hair asks, "Is it true?"

"Is what true?" I snap back.

"That you spent the week in rehab?"

"What? No, I didn't. Who the hell said that?"

"Your friend Candace."

They walk off and I fall back against my locker. *Everyone thinks that I spent the week in rehab?* Why is Candace spreading these rumours? My legs feel weak, but I step away from the safety of my locker and go in search of Candace. I need to find out what happened.

I spot the girls in the canteen area getting some breakfast. There are a few other people around, but I keep walking straight up to their table. Samuel and his friends are with the girls. He has his arm around Candace and they are making out. I clear my throat, gaining everyone's attention. I swallow back the lump.

I can't chicken out now. I need answers. "What's going on? Why didn't you message me after the show? And what's the go with the rumours too?"

Candace pulls back and stares right through me. "'Cause of you, our parents found out what happened, and we got grounded. It's all 'cause you can't hold your liquor and made a complete fool of yourself. If you didn't spend the week at rehab, maybe you should. You need to sort out your drinking problem."

All the colour drains from my face and I feel the tears forming, but I don't

dare fall apart. Not yet. Candace starts talking to the girls as if I'm not there anymore. I look to Ashley. She smiles in apology, but she doesn't stick up for me. I turn and quickly walk away. I don't stop until I'm in the girls' toilets. I lock myself in a cubical and the tears drop. My body collapses to the ground.

Is it true? Do I have a drinking problem? She said that I made a complete fool of myself. I wish I had a video of what happened that night just so I could know.

The door to the toilets opens and girls' voices fill the room. I don't dare move a muscle. Then I hear Candace's voice.

"She is such a fucking loser. How dare she come up to me and question me about the rumours when she's the one who caused them?"

"Yeah, total loser," Lee pipes up.

My heart feels like it's about to burst. I want to scream or punch something. I need to get out of here. Time seems to stop as I wait for them to leave. As soon as the door click shut, I leave my cubical and run straight out of the toilets. I don't stop until I reach my place.

Luckily, no one is home. I slam my bedroom door shut and collapse to the ground. Why are girls so cruel? I wish they understood that I just made a mistake. I didn't mean to muck up. If I could take it all back, I would.

Daring Support

If you too are struggling with what Sophie has gone through please seek professional help as soon as possible, you don't have to go through this by yourself. There are support systems out there that can listen, support and offer professional advice.

Please refer to page 261 for more information.

Friendship check-in

True friends—they are hard to come by. You may think you're alone but trust me, your true friends are out there. They will come into your life when you least expect it.

Find friends who will stick with you through thick and thin. If you make a huge mistake, you want to know that your friends will be there with you, holding you while you cry. They will tell you that yeah, you stuffed up, but we all do. It's a part of living and learning. We all make mistakes so that we can learn from them.

Daring Culture: True Friends

> How should a friend respond to this situation that Sophie has found herself in?

"What's going on? Why didn't you message me after the show? And what's the go with the rumours too?"

"'Cause of you, our parents found out what happened, and we got grounded. It's all 'cause you can't hold your liquor and made a complete fool of yourself. If you didn't spend the week at rehab, maybe you should. You need to sort out your drinking problem."

> A true friend might say this instead:

"We got grounded because of what **we** did that night. But we all got in shit and it isn't your fault."

Daring Movement: #squadgoals

> How many of these have you done, or do you do with your best friend? How many can you tick off?

- ☐ Taken a road trip
- ☐ Can be yourselves around each other
- ☐ Movie marathon
- ☐ Travelled abroad
- ☐ Got manicures
- ☐ Owned matching jewellery
- ☐ Can say what you really think
- ☐ 2 a.m. texting
- ☐ Made a time capsule
- ☐ Planned out your futures together
- ☐ Regular tags in memes
- ☐ Sent selfies
- ☐ Raided each other's fridges
- ☐ Shared song
- ☐ Pulled an all-nighter
- ☐ Made up a dance routine
- ☐ Tried a DIY together
- ☐ Swapped names
- ☐ Known each other's secrets
- ☐ Been on holidays together
- ☐ Wore matching outfits
- ☐ Been there for each other through a rough time
- ☐ Created a photo collage
- ☐ Spoken a secret language
- ☐ Had a pamper day
- ☐ Called each other's parents your own
- ☐ Shared clothes

Your best friend score ___/27

Wearing a Mask

Friendship isn't about being there when it's convenient.

It's about being there always, even when times are tough.

Things in common check-in

Find friends who you have common interests with. I used to make friends when I was out drinking at parties but then I realised that the only thing we had in common was drinking. Which isn't ideal, because every time we hung out it had to involve alcohol. But when you find friends who you have something in common with—let's say some type of sport, or a sense of humour for example—then you'll have fun playing together and the friendship will develop from shared interests.

Daring Movement: Making New Friends

Conversation starters for making new friends:

- What did you do today?
- What's your favourite sport?
- What do you do when you're not at school?
- What's your favourite TV show?
- How many brothers and sisters do you have?
- What do you want to do when you grow up?
- What are you reading?
- What's your favourite food?
- What's your best subject at school?
- What subject do you hate at school?
- Do you like dogs or cats?
- Do you have a pet?
- What are you doing on the weekend?
- Where would you like to travel to?

Wearing a Mask

Daring Culture: Types of Friends

Friends you need in your life:

The cheer squad
Someone who yells and screams for you from the sidelines. Those friends who cheer you on and encourage you through your wins and your losses.

The driver
A friend who always pushes you to do better. They make you step outside of your comfort zone; they help you smash your goals. They help you be the best version of yourself that you can be.

The loyal amigo
Someone who is always by your side no matter what. If you're feeling down, they will be there the second you tell them you're upset. They will hold your hand and listen to your every word.

The booster
That energetic friend who always keeps you on your toes. The one who is always encouraging you to dream big and set those giant, scary goals. They are full of energy and their enthusiasm rubs off on you.

The mentor
A friend who you look up to. Someone who is wise and has accomplished what you wish to achieve. A person who you can gain experience from and who can offer you worldly advice.

The daring sidekick
Someone who makes you step outside of your comfort zone. They go with you on crazy adventures and you have the best fun with them. They aren't afraid of anything which is a breath of fresh air.

The hilarious (wild) friend
Someone who makes you laugh until your tummy hurts. They entertain you and make you smile when you think that you can't.

The best friend
This person is everything; your cheer squad, the driver, the loyal amigo, the booster, the mentor, the daring sidekick, and the hilarious friend. This person is the one who you will grow with throughout your life.

Daring Movement: Your Ideal Friend

Describe your ideal friend.

Personality:

Traits:

Things in common:

How do you want them to make you feel:

Surround yourself with your people—Those who you can't stop talking with.

The ones who laugh and cry with you.

They are YOUR people.

Drinking check-in

As she mentions here, Sophie believes that alcohol gives her the confidence to be herself without having to wear her mask.

'The drinks give me this confidence that I can just be who I want to be. Who I really am.'

> Sophie can be herself without having to drink. It's about having the confidence to be who you really are. Alcohol shouldn't be used as a magic medicine to make you feel brave. You can be who you are always. Using alcohol is just an excuse to drop the mask that you may have put up.

Daring Culture: Substance Abuse

We use substances for a lot of reasons. Some of them may be:

♥ **To forget about someone who hurt you or a painful situation.**
Drugs or alcohol may numb the pain in that moment, but you will still remember the heartache the next day and it will probably feel ten times worse with that killer hangover.

♥ **To relax and let off steam after a bad day.**
It may be your way to relax after a stressful day but finding a more natural approach may be more beneficial in the long run. You could instead try going for a walk in the fresh air, relaxing in a fragrant bath, watching your favourite TV series or movie, calling a friend to talk about your day, reading a good book to clear your mind, or making something.

♥ **To give you confidence.**
This is something that I struggled with—using alcohol as a way to be myself. It worked in the moment but then the next day I'd regret it when I'd hear what I'd done. And the hangover killed me! I thought that I needed the magic drink to be myself, but it's totally not the case. You can be yourself in every situation and in front of anyone. It's about learning who you are and owning the shit out of that.

♥ **To be someone you're not.**
Why would you want to be someone you're not? You're a unique human being, a limited edition. Own It. Be who you want to be, who you love. You know how your best friends describe you to someone? You may cringe, thinking *I'm so not that cool*. But you are that cool. Think of yourself as your best friend would. Describe what you love about yourself and your best assets. Give yourself a pep talk when those negative thoughts creep in. Fight them off with the opposite of what they are saying.

> **Example:**
> Voice in your head: *You're stupid.*
> Switch it to: *You're smart.*
> Voice in your head: *I failed maths, I'm not good enough.*
> Switch it to: *I may have failed math, but I'm really good at English.*

♥ **To have fun.**
Alcohol can definitely add some fun to a party, but you don't need to drink to have fun. Remember when you were ten years old and you had slumber parties with your friends? You pulled all-nighters without even a sip of alcohol. You had the best time, didn't you? Think of this when you go out to a party—you can still have fun. Don't think that you have to keep drinking just because everyone else is. You can also pretend that your cup is full of alcohol but really, it's just a soft drink.

♥ **To fit in.**

Your true, real friends won't care if you don't drink. They will still invite you to the party because they want you to be there. You don't have to just because your friends are and because you may stand out if you don't. Have your own voice and say you're not drinking tonight. Some friends may think that's lame but just stand up for yourself.

> You could say, "I don't want to drink tonight."
> Or "I've got to get up early tomorrow for something."
> Or "Nah, I don't need to drink."
>
> See how easy that was?
> You can develop a script of what response you will have beforehand. So that way you are prepared and won't feel uncomfortable. You've got this!

Daring Movement: Who Am I?

> Self-discovery is essential to your confidence and individuality.
> Get to know yourself.

Ask yourself, "Who am I?"

Who do you want to be?

What do you fear most about being yourself?

What is the one failure that you have turned into your greatest lesson?

Daring Journey

Write a story about the best day you've had.

Wearing a Mask

You don't need any magic serum to be who you really are.

Raise that head of yours, darling. Show the world how amazing you are.

A love letter to my teenage self
by Jenna Lee

Jenna is a USA Today Bestselling Author, youth mentor, and creator at heart. You can find out more about her here www.jennalee.biz

Dear Jenna,

I know you're **hurting**. You've locked yourself in your room. You're screaming and refusing to go back to school after all the heartache. Trust me, **things will get better**.

Don't let anyone bring you down, not now, not ever. Lift that pretty little head of yours and show them that what they say and do doesn't affect you. You want to know why they bully you? Why they say those mean things? Because they are struggling with their own issues that have nothing to do with you whatsoever. And they don't know how to deal with their insecurities, so they take it out on you and others who they feel threatened by. I'm not saying it's right, not at all, but you are so much **stronger** than you realise; you just don't know it yet.

Stay strong, **beautiful girl**. Smile brightly, and don't hold back. The sooner you realise your worth, the better. Discover your strengths and your weaknesses. Search for those people who get you, the ones you can be your **True self** around without putting on your mask. That mask disguises who you really are, and you're **so much better** than that, Jenna. Don't waste all these years pretending to be this girl you're not. Because after school is over, you won't be hanging with this crowd anymore. You will have realised that these people, they aren't your people; they're just peers you went to high school with. So please, **Trust your instincts** and be yourself. That beautiful, bubbly, creative, girl is perfect just as she is, and one day, she's going to **change the world.**

Be brave. Those negative voices in your head are overwhelming, but they aren't telling you the truth. They are far from it. I know you think they are right, and that you're a mess, and that life isn't worth living. But, I'm here to tell you differently. Everything IS going to be **okay**. You're going to grow into the most incredible woman who is so kind, smart, beautiful, and **Talented**. You have so much to give. Don't shy away; not now, not ever. Be yourself, always. You may find that some people won't like you, and that's okay too.

We aren't meant to like everyone in the world, but you will find your people—the ones who support you no matter what, and who alone will tell you the truth. Trust your parents. They are **amazing**, and will always have your best interests at **heart** (even though right now they're telling you that you can't go to that party). Stop giving them such a hard time. You think it's unfair that everyone is going, and that if you don't go, you won't be cool, but you know what? They're looking out for you because they **love** you so much, and they've probably already realised that this crowd of people you've been hanging around aren't your people.

Now get out of your dark room, get outside, and scream this to the world:

"**I am enough.** I am fucking beautiful, and I won't let anyone, including myself, bring me down."

Lots of **love**,

Your older self x

I'm not beautiful like you.
I'm beautiful like me.

I'm Not Beautiful Like You

Lying on my bed, I flick through a fashion magazine. I stop looking at a vibrant page that catches my attention, it's an image of a model. I stare, taking in every detail, from her face that looks flawless, to her straight silky hair, to her tiny and tanned arms. She's wearing a black and white polka-dot dress that hugs her body flawlessly. Her boobs look to be the right size—not too big or too small, just right. Her stomach is flat down to her thin legs. Everything about her screams perfection.

I should look the same. I get off my bed and walk over to my mirror. I hate what I see in the reflection. Why can't I look like the model in the magazine?

I'm not pretty.

I'm not skinny. I'm overweight.

My arms aren't thin like hers; they are flabbier.

My face isn't flawless like hers. It's covered in pimples.

My legs aren't toned like hers. They have stretch marks.

I look nothing like her and I should. She's normal, what I'm supposed to look like. My legs give out and I fall to the ground. Clutching my arms around myself, I rock back and forth, letting my tears fall down my cheeks.

It's not fair. *Why can't I be normal?* No wonder no one wants to go out with me. Because I don't look like her.

"Eddie, sweetie, you're going to be late," my mother yells.

Giving myself one last look in the mirror, I plaster on a fake smile and get

I'm Not Beautiful Like You

ready for school. After a quick shower, I keep my hair down. My ugly curls cover my cheeks. I put on a thick layer of makeup but it doesn't help me. My jeans feel tight against my skin and my tummy rolls over the waistband. I turn away from the mirror, unable to look at myself for a second longer.

My mother's in the kitchen and she passes me my lunch bag. I take it from her, smiling and kissing her goodbye.

Like nothing's wrong. Like I'm not screaming inside.

Instead, I walk away, meeting my dad at his car.

"Have a great day, sweetie," Mum yells from the door. I wave back at her as I close it.

My dad talks on the way to school about a football game on the weekend, complaining about his team. I sit in silence the entire trip.

After he drops me off, I stuff my lunch into my bag. My morning classes are a blur. Lunch comes around and I sit with my friends on the grass. They aren't eating their lunch, only snacking on healthy fruit. I glance at the chicken and salad sandwich in my hand. My stomach rumbles but her body appears in my mind. I think of the rolls on my stomach. I shake my head as I walk over to the bin and chuck my sandwich away.

I make my way back to my friends and sit down quietly. No one says a word and for that I'm grateful. I don't feel like explaining myself to anyone. I desperately want to look like her, the girl in the magazine, even if it means being hungry.

After lunch, I have two classes. Throughout the whole last lesson, I can't concentrate. Everything the teacher is saying is going in one ear and out the other. All I can think about is my rumbling stomach. I tell it to shut up several times, but it won't listen. By the time my mother picks me up from school, I have no energy left. I shuffle my legs to her car and hop in.

She looks me over and frowns. "You feeling okay, sweetie?"

My heart starts to pound faster. She can't find out that I chucked out her lunch she would kill me for wasting food. I quickly come up with a lie. "Yeah fine, Mum. Just feeling a bit off; that's all," I say, and glance out the window.

I hate lying to my mum, but she wouldn't understand, and I don't want to worry her. She has enough on her plate with work. It's no big deal anyway.

The next few weeks, I chuck out my lunch every day. It becomes a habit.

Things get bad.

I have to eat my dinner in front of Mum and Dad, and it makes me feel like shit. It's making me put on weight when all I want to do is lose it. I eat as much as I can stomach and beg my mum to let me finish. I've been playing the whole sick card as to why I've lost my appetite.

I'm now staring at myself in my mirror. I don't look any different. I still look fat and ugly. Not like her. I can't stand to see myself any longer. I slam my wardrobe door shut and fall to my bed. I feel so weak. Everything has been a struggle lately.

"Eddie, dinner is ready," my mother yells.

I let out a sigh. *Great, another meal that will add more rolls to my stomach.* I drag myself down the hallway and into the kitchen.

Mum's dishing up spaghetti. I almost vomit at the sight. I'm not hungry. Dad takes our bowls and places them on the kitchen table.

"We need to book you in to see the doctor, sweetie. It's been weeks now and you've been unwell. You haven't been eating. You'll soon fade away to nothing," Mum says, as I take a small bite of pasta.

The taste hits my tongue and I hold back a gag. What does she mean I'll fade away to nothing? I'm overweight.

"I've had a virus, Mum. I'll be fine." I smile but I see the worry in her eyes.

She shakes her head and looks to my father for support.

"Your mother's right, Eddie. You haven't been yourself lately."

"I said I'm fine," I snap. "I've had enough," I say, after a few mouthfuls. I push back my bowl.

"No, you need to eat more." My father raises his voice.

Shaking my head, I push my chair away and walk to the bathroom.

"Get back here now, Eddie. You're not finished."

"I am," I scream and slam the bathroom door shut.

I lock it and fall to my hands and knees. My body starts to shake. I crawl over to the shower and pull the lever. I slowly take off my clothes, then step in. The water falls all around me, the droplets prick my skin. They feel like needles stinging me.

My legs give out and I fall to the ground.

Fists bang against the bathroom door, but I ignore them.

"Eddie, open this door now," my father growls.

I lean over, my hand on the cold tile wall. My fingers find their way down my throat and I make myself throw up my dinner until there's nothing left. It feels good knowing there isn't anything there. I lean back against the wall, water dripping down my body as I sit here and sway back and forth. I keep telling myself it will be worth it, that I will look like her.

Weeks turn into months, and my parents start to ask more and more questions, begging me to talk to them. But I refuse, until one day when my mum and dad sit me down.

My mother has tears in her eyes and it hits me that I'm causing them pain.

"What's going on with you? You have lost so much weight. Please tell us. Let us help?"

My mother breaks down. Then I look to my father and he too has tears in his eyes.

Why are they so concerned? I haven't lost any weight. I still don't look like her.

My mother comes around the table and takes my hand before leading me to the bathroom. The room begins to spin. I pull back my hand and stop to catch my breath. I fall to the ground, unable to hold my own weight. Everything is plunged into darkness.

Loud beeping fills my ears. I open my eyes to find that I'm not at home anymore. I glance around at the crisp white walls that surround me. The sterile smell of cleaning products hit my nose and I know that I'm in a hospital.

My parents are next to me; my mother's holding my hand. A doctor walks in carrying a clipboard. I must have fainted. The doctor smiles at my parents and Mum squeezes my hand tighter.

"Eddie, you're lucky your parents brought you in when they did. Do you understand why you've been admitted?" He looks at me and I shrink farther into the sheets.

I turn towards my mother and father. They both look upset. I shake my head at the doctor. "Because I fainted?" I mumble.

"Yes. Do you know why you fainted?"

"I have no idea," I answer honestly.

"Eddie, you have lost a lot of weight in a short period of time. Do you want to tell me about that?"

My stomach sinks as I hear his words. *But I still don't look like her.* He's lying. I look to my mum for help. So, she can tell him he's wrong. Tears fall down her cheeks.

"Honey, it's true. I don't think you can see yourself as we do, but you have lost a lot of weight," my mother says, wiping her tears away.

I let go of her hand and push down the sheets covering me. I'm dressed in a white nightgown. I look at my body.

Just seconds ago, I saw fat arms, not like hers.

A fat tummy, not like hers, and large legs, not like hers.

But now as I really look, I see bones sticking out from my skin. I see no fat anywhere.

I feel weak.

Tears fall over my cheeks and I break down in my mother's arms. What did I do to myself? Just because I wanted to look like her?

Daring Support

If you too are struggling with what Eddie has gone through you don't have to go through this by yourself. Eddie went on to get help from her doctor, counsellor and had great support systems in place to help her get through. If you are feeling similar, please seek professional help as soon as possible. There are support systems out there that can listen, support and offer professional advice.

Please refer to page 261 for more information.

Comparison check-in

For Eddie we can see that she was triggered by comparison, comparison is something that we go to do every time we see someone. It's a habit to check the person out and compare them to yourself. But it's important to remember that you don't need to compare yourself to anyone else. You are PERFECT just the way you are, and you know what? The person you're comparing yourself to is most likely doing the exact same thing with you.

You don't need to change one single thing about yourself. You can love yourself just like everyone else around you does. Be happy in your own skin. Show yourself love and support, just like you would to your friend.

We are all unique human beings. None of us are exactly the same and that's so beautiful. We all have different body types and personalities. Can you imagine if we looked and acted the same? That would be totally boring. Let's be who we really are.

A Daring Mantra

Be you.
Love the way you talk, walk, and act.

Be you.
Embrace your uniqueness and quirks.

Be you.
Hold your head high and walk with confidence.

Be you.
Don't second-guess your actions—just be you.

into the sheets.

I turn towards my mother and father. They both look upset. I shake my head at the doctor. "Because I fainted?" I mumble.

"Yes. Do you know why you fainted?"

"I have no idea," I answer honestly.

"Eddie, you have lost a lot of weight in a short period of time. Do you want to tell me about that?"

My stomach sinks as I hear his words. *But I still don't look like her.* He's lying. I look to my mum for help. So, she can tell him he's wrong. Tears fall down her cheeks.

"Honey, it's true. I don't think you can see yourself as we do, but you have lost a lot of weight," my mother says, wiping her tears away.

I let go of her hand and push down the sheets covering me. I'm dressed in a white nightgown. I look at my body.

Just seconds ago, I saw fat arms, not like hers.

A fat tummy, not like hers, and large legs, not like hers.

But now as I really look, I see bones sticking out from my skin. I see no fat anywhere.

I feel weak.

Tears fall over my cheeks and I break down in my mother's arms. What did I do to myself? Just because I wanted to look like her?

Daring Support

If you too are struggling with what Eddie has gone through you don't have to go through this by yourself. Eddie went on to get help from her doctor, counsellor and had great support systems in place to help her get through. If you are feeling similar, please seek professional help as soon as possible. There are support systems out there that can listen, support and offer professional advice.

Please refer to page 261 for more information.

Comparison check-in

For Eddie we can see that she was triggered by comparison, comparison is something that we go to do every time we see someone. It's a habit to check the person out and compare them to yourself. But it's important to remember that you don't need to compare yourself to anyone else. You are PERFECT just the way you are, and you know what? The person you're comparing yourself to is most likely doing the exact same thing with you.

You don't need to change one single thing about yourself. You can love yourself just like everyone else around you does. Be happy in your own skin. Show yourself love and support, just like you would to your friend.

We are all unique human beings. None of us are exactly the same and that's so beautiful. We all have different body types and personalities. Can you imagine if we looked and acted the same? That would be totally boring. Let's be who we really are.

A Daring Mantra

Be you.
Love the way you talk, walk, and act.

Be you.
Embrace your uniqueness and quirks.

Be you.
Hold your head high and walk with confidence.

Be you.
Don't second-guess your actions—just be you.

Daring Culture: Accepting Compliments

Do you ever get a compliment from a friend, maybe that your legs look great in a dress? How did you react to the compliment?

I know when I used to get compliments, I would get embarrassed and say, "Nah, no way."

But now, I own it and I let the compliment wash over me, and I accept it fully. Smiling, I reply, "Thank you."

Daring Movement: Love Your Body

> Learn to love your body.
> Example: I love my **smile** because it's **beautiful**.

I love my _____ because _____
I love my _____ because _____
I love my _____ because _____
I love my _____ because _____
I love my _____ because _____
I love my _____ because _____
I love my _____ because _____
I love my _____ because _____
I love my _____ because _____

I'm Not Beautiful Like You

We can't love others until we learn to love ourselves first.

Beauty is about loving who you are, and accepting and loving the body you have been blessed with. It's about being comfortable with what you've got.

Daring Culture: Advertising & Media

You know these models who we see in the magazines and on social media? They aren't real. Well yes, the model is real, but the photograph isn't true-to-life. After it's captured, it's edited with filters, and body parts are trimmed, cut, and perfected. The final product you see isn't one hundred percent real. Remember this next time you compare yourself to models on social media and in magazines. They are really just like you: naturally beautiful in their own ways.

Daring Culture: Stop Comparing

How to stop comparing yourself to others:

♥ **Catch yourself**
We all have those moments where we think, 'Oh I wish I could look like that'. The important thing is to catch yourself when you think it. Don't let it bring you down.

♥ **Flip the compliment**
When you've done the above and caught yourself, the next step is to flip your thoughts around. Switch them to compliment yourself too. See below example:

'Oh, she looks flawless. That dress looks amazing on her.'

My initial thought: 'I couldn't pull it off.'
Flip it: 'Just like I would too. My body would be bangin' in that dress.'

Daring Movement: Flip It

> It's your turn to flip Eddie's thoughts on what she thinks she sees in the mirror.

Why can't I look like the model in the magazine? > *Because it's not real.*

I'm not pretty. > *I am pretty.*

My arms aren't thin like hers. They are flabbier. > *My arms are perfect the way they are.*

I'm not skinny, I'm overweight. > _____

_____

My face isn't flawless, like hers. It's covered in pimples. > _____

_____

My legs aren't toned, like hers. They have stretch marks. > _____

_____

I look nothing like her, and I should. She's normal, what I'm supposed to look like. > _____

_____

Daring Movement: Love Your Body

> This is a page of gratitude.
> Draw or write what you love most about your body.

I'm Not Beautiful Like You

Real girls aren't perfect.

Perfect girls aren't real.

Self-love check-in

I once thought that if I loved myself fully, I would be one of those arrogant people who I didn't like. But the only reason I didn't like them is because I wished I could be like them: confident. So happy and strong in my own skin that it would shine right out of me. I would carry myself with so much confidence.

It all starts from within—giving yourself compliments and accepting your friends' compliments.

I always use this trick when practicing self-love. I pretend that I'm my own best friend. What would my best friend say about me? She would say that I'm kind, beautiful, talented, and amazing. See how easy that is?

Have you ever had one of those days when you felt so good in your own skin? When you skipped around your house, singing your fave tune, and you just feel fantastic? I want you to feel like that every single day because you deserve that. You deserve to feel like you could take on the world.

> **Things to remember:**
> *You are beautiful inside and out.*
> *Having a bad day is normal.*
> *It's okay to ask for help.*
> *Love yourself with everything you have.*

Self-love is the most important thing that we can teach ourselves and continue to do each day. It's about listening to your body, mind, and spirit, and asking yourself how you feel, what you want, and what you need. Doing something for yourself that lights you up without feeling any guilt for doing it. Listening to your body when it's sore, vegging out, eating junk food, and binge-watching your fave movies because you listened to yourself. It's about hanging out with your friends because you want to. Listening to yourself and giving yourself exactly what you need without making excuses.

I'm Not Beautiful Like You

I want you to look in the mirror.
See that beautiful lady
staring back at you?

She wants you to tell her every day
that she's amazing, so beautiful, and
that she can achieve anything
she puts her mind to.

Can you do that for her?

Daring Culture: Affirmations

> Positive affirmations to say in front of the mirror:

- ♥ I am beautiful.
- ♥ I am courageous.
- ♥ I am mindful.
- ♥ I am powerful.
- ♥ I am kind.
- ♥ I am confident.
- ♥ I am creative.
- ♥ I am compassionate.
- ♥ I am determined.
- ♥ I am daring.

From the positive affirmations deck by 'Shining Your Light'

Daring Culture: Me Time

> Ideas for things to do when you need time to yourself:

- ♥ Listen to music
- ♥ Write in a journal
- ♥ Watch a movie
- ♥ Draw a picture
- ♥ Colour in
- ♥ Go for a walk
- ♥ Read a book
- ♥ Paint your nails
- ♥ Have a facial
- ♥ Call a friend
- ♥ Visit a friend
- ♥ Play sport
- ♥ Meditate
- ♥ Cook something

I'm Not Beautiful Like You

Daring Movement: A Kind Quote

A quote I live by.
Come up with a quote to stick up on your mirror.
Something kind to repeat every day.

Daring Movement: Me

Get to know me:

Name

Age

My hobbies

Natural hair colour

Eye colour

What I love most about me

Favourite food

I love to

I wish I knew more about

I love my

I am grateful for

I am

I'm Not Beautiful Like You

She loved herself so much that others' opinions started to fade away into nothing.

Daring Movement: A Love Letter To Me

Write yourself a love letter.

Dear ...

I love you, because ...

I'm Not Beautiful Like You

The strongest girls know who they are and what they believe in.

A love letter to my teenage self
by Sabine McKenzie

Sabine is a speaker, recovery mentor, and youth mentor. You can find out more about her here www.sabinemckenzie.com.au/

Dear Sabine,

I know you feel that you know best. You have all the **answers**. You are at that point where no one can tell you otherwise. You are **smart**, strong-willed, and dedicated. When you aim for the stars, most of the time you get the moon as well. I still admire these **qualities** in you.

But, I also know that inside you are **hurting**. You are trying to please. Make people happy. Make people proud.

You are a chameleon, changing your colours to not just survive, but thrive in your surroundings.

I understand that you do this because sometimes you feel inadequate. Not pretty enough. Not smart enough. Not thin enough. **Not enough.**

I understand that your answer to this is to be better. Do better. Keep striving. Keep thriving. Thinner. Fitter. Smarter.

Sabine, your **worth** is not found in your weight, your image, or your accolades. You need not be a chameleon. You need not change your colours. You don't need to start that punishing exercise regime. You don't need to starve **yourself**.

Your worth is in the **love** you give. The **kindness** you bring. The curiosity you show. The eagerness you display.

Your worth is in the words you write. The people you help. The **difference you make**.

Your worth is in your determination. Your **strength** to not give up. Your power to overcome an eating disorder. To overcome depression. To choose to live. To redefine **beauty**.

Beauty isn't one image. It's all of us. Different sizes. Colours. Abilities. Genders. The media doesn't do a great job of showing it—but if you look for it, I promise you will find it.

Beauty isn't what your body looks like. It's what your body can do. Walk. Talk. Eat. Play. Laugh. Cry. Cook. Clean. Study. Sport. Hold hands. Jump. Kiss. As Taryn Brumfitt will later teach you, "your body is a vessel, not an ornament".

Because really, **beauty is undefined**. It's asking for help. It's understanding your values. It's embracing your imperfections. It's appreciating those who **love you** for you. It's speaking up for injustice. It's asking questions. It's making mistakes. It's seeing everyone as equal. It's actioning change. It's feeling all the emotions. It's owning your worth. It's sharing your heart. **It's being grateful.**

Sabine, I don't have all the answers. But I do know this... you are the stars. You are the moon. You are capable. You are loved.

You are enough.

Lots of **love,**

Your older self x

And she finally gave up.

She dropped the fake smile and whispered to herself, "I can't do this anymore."

I Can't do This Anymore

It has been a bad week; my friends are ignoring me. Everyone hates me at school. The only time I can be myself is when I get drunk at parties. But I ruined that too over the weekend. I got so drunk that I once again blacked out. I can't remember a thing from the night. What did I do? What happened?

I've heard rumours that apparently, I was dancing on someone's kitchen table and I hooked up with Sam. How could I be so stupid? I bet everyone is talking about me, calling me names. I'm the laughing stock of school. And apparently, I'm 'easy' now. I've got guys messaging me, wanting to 'hang out'.

I push my face farther into my pillow and I scream as loud as I possibly can. I scream at myself for being so stupid, for making myself a target for all these messages and rumours. It's all my fault. The pillow silences my screams, which I'm grateful for.

A loud knock on my door has me sitting upright and wiping away my tears. My mother peeks her head around my door. Concern is written all over her face. I don't make eye contact; afraid she will know that something is wrong. I can't handle her pity.

"What's going on? You okay?" she asks.

This is exactly what I didn't want to happen.

"I'm fine, Mum. Just leave me alone," I yell, turning over and giving her my shoulder.

She won't understand; she doesn't know what it's like. She's still here, but

I Can't do This Anymore

I don't turn around, she will see right through me. I'm frightened that she will find out everything—that I'm a complete screw-up. The bed dips and she rubs her hand over my back. Tears fall down my cheeks, but I still hide away from her, hoping she won't see.

"I'm here if you need to talk," she says.

"Just leave me alone," I mumble.

She embraces me quickly and releases me. She leaves me, closing the door behind her. Instantly, I feel cold and wish she would come back. But I know she won't because I've pushed her away like I do with everyone I love. I need to make myself hurt for all the damage I have caused. The shame I have brought on myself.

I have to make myself feel the pain.

Rubbing away my tears, I move over to my desk in search of something that will help ease my agony. Something that will make me pay for my stupid behaviour. I deserve to be punished. I deserve to hurt. I find what I need, then I make my way back to my bed.

I sit, pushing up my hoodie sleeves. I look at the scars that line my wrists. They should stop me but instead, they remind me of the other times I've mucked up. I need to make myself pay again. It's my way of releasing the tension even if it only lasts a second. My scars remind me of a time when I didn't know how else to release the heartache.

Daring Support

If you too are struggling with what Sara has gone through please seek professional help as soon as possible, you don't have to go through this by yourself. There are support systems out there that can listen, support and offer professional advice.

Please refer to page 261 for more information.

Self-care check-in

You may get to a point in your life when you think that there's no other way. That you have to make yourself pay; you have to physically feel the pain. I have scars that line my wrists and they are a reminder of a time when I lost control. A time in my life when I thought there was no other way out. But I'm here to tell you that there IS another way. You don't need to hurt yourself to deal with the hard moments. Trust me, I've been in dark places too. But I wish I had opened up to someone. A friend, my family—I wish I'd told anyone how I was feeling so that I didn't inflict pain upon myself.

You may be going through this now, have experienced it in the past, or have thought about it. Just stop. Stop and find another way to release your heartache. There are a million ways to deal with what you're feeling right now. We are going to talk about some solutions in the pages that follow. Remember, you are not alone; we are in this together.

We spend too much of our lives running around, keeping 'busy' and 'doing'. Instead, we should be stopping and asking ourselves what we need. What do we need to continue on? We often forget to ask ourselves this simple question that will help us tremendously.

I know there are going to be moments in your life that will change your path. You will make huge mistakes and you'll think that your life is over. You will learn from those hard experiences. They will shape you into the woman you will become. Let them make you stronger, smarter, confident, and kinder. Scream, cry and let it all out. Then lift your head high and move forward.

This letter is to you.

I know you're hurting, I feel it too, but I want you to get out of bed. Open your curtains and smile.

Smile for the air in your lungs.
Smile for the place you live.
Smile for the heart you've got.
Smile for the beautiful face you have.
Smile for the loving family you have.
Smile for being here in this moment.
Smile for the love you have.
Smile because today is a new day with new possibilities.

Now take a deep breath
and lift that pretty little head of yours.

You've got this.

Daring Culture: Self-care ideas

- ♥ Read
- ♥ Go outside for a walk
- ♥ Journal
- ♥ Call a friend
- ♥ Hang out with a family member
- ♥ Listen to music
- ♥ Colour in
- ♥ Go for a run, sweat it out
- ♥ Draw
- ♥ Play with your pet
- ♥ Watch a movie
- ♥ Go for a swim
- ♥ Ask someone for help, talk to your parents.

> Can't talk to them? A counsellor at school. Can't talk there? Here's Beyond Blue's number 1300 224 636

Daring Movement: Self-care checklist

- ☐ Got out of bed
- ☐ Did my hair
- ☐ Looked at myself in the mirror, practiced my daily affirmations and smiled
- ☐ Treated myself
- ☐ Did something I'm passionate about
- ☐ Talked to someone I love
- ☐ Relaxed and had downtime with myself
- ☐ Hugged someone
- ☐ Danced to a song I love
- ☐ Listened to my body
- ☐ Laughed
- ☐ Eaten nourishingly
- ☐ Moved my body

I Can't do This Anymore

Self-care isn't selfish.

Daring Movement: Seven-day Self-care challenge

1 Go for a walk in nature ☐	**2** Take a bath ☐
3 Start reading a new book ☐	**4** Draw a picture ☐
5 Meditate for ten minutes ☐	**6** Paint your nails ☐
7 Journal about your week ☐	

I Can't do This Anymore

Self-care is about giving yourself all the love you deserve.

Daring Movement: Your Mood

Draw your current mood:

I Can't do This Anymore

Daring Movement: Getting To Know You

> **Let's get to know you.**
> Write down what books, songs, and movies you always go back to.
> The never-fail things that make you smile, no matter what.

Books:

Songs:

Movies, TV shows:

Reaching out check-in

One of the bravest things you can do is reach out and ask for help. Tell your parents or a loved one that you're not okay, you are struggling. You don't have to go into details—just let them know. A huge weight will be lifted from your shoulders.

You shouldn't have to carry all the pain by yourself. You deserve to feel one hundred percent and get the support you need.

Daring Culture: Reaching Out

My mother peeks her head around my door. Concern is written all over her face. I don't make eye contact; afraid she will know that something is wrong. I can't handle her pity.

"What's going on? You okay?" she asks.

This is exactly what I didn't want to happen.

"I'm fine, Mum. Just leave me alone," I yell, turning over and giving her my shoulder.

She won't understand; she doesn't know what it's like. She's still here, but I don't turn around, she will see right through me. I'm frightened that she will find out everything—that I'm a complete screw-up. The bed dips and she rubs her hand over my back. Tears fall down my cheeks, but I still hide away from her, hoping she won't see.

> Sadie could have been honest with her mother.
> Let's see how it could have played out differently.

My mother peeks her head around my door. Concern is written all over her face. I don't make eye contact; afraid she will know that something is wrong. I

You can't find your voice unless you learn to use it first.

can't handle her pity.

"What's going on? You okay?" she asks.

This is exactly what I didn't want to happen. She stays there. She doesn't say anything, just rubbing circles on my back.

"If you want to talk..." she says.

She won't get what's happening to me, the agony inside my soul. But what if she does? I pause.

"I'm not okay," I yell, turning over and giving her my shoulder.

Maybe she'll understand. She might know what it's like.

She's still here, but I don't turn around, she will see right through me. I'm frightened that she will find out everything—that I'm a complete screw-up. The bed dips and she rubs her hand over my back. Tears fall down my cheeks, but I still hide away from her, hoping she won't see. "I'm here if you need to talk," she says.

"I'm not coping, Mum. Everyone at school hates me," I mumble.

"I'm sure they don't, sweetie. But if you need to talk to someone about it, I can arrange that. Just let me know."

I consider her words.

"Aren't counsellors only for crazy people?"

"Of course not, a lot of people go there to just talk. To let off steam."

Maybe it will be easier to talk to someone other than my family.

"Yeah, Mum, I think I'd like that." I turn around to face her and she embraces me in a hug.

> Now Sadie has someone to talk to; she isn't alone.

Reaching Out check-in 2.0

Being honest is the best thing you can do. If someone asks you if you are okay, reply honestly. We are too used to plastering on a fake smile and saying everything's fine. It's time to be open and tell the truth.

Talking to a counsellor can be very powerful: a complete stranger who doesn't know you or hold any judgment. I went to see a counsellor when I was around sixteen or seventeen, but I made a mistake. I literally sat in every session and didn't talk. I looked at her with judgment. I thought *why would she care? She doesn't know me.* But now, looking back it's one thing I regret because all those excuses are actually positives. I'd rather talk to a stranger and let it all out to them rather than to someone I love. Yes, the counsellor doesn't know me and that's amazing. I can tell her everything. I can spill my heart, my deepest and darkest thoughts, because I'm not worried that it will change a meaningful relationship. They aren't my family. They will offer the best advice a stranger can give because they're not connected to me as a loved one. To find a counsellor you can through https://au.reachout.com/ or you can also call a help line on 1800 55 1800.

You may have a friend who you really trust—one who just listens or offers the best advice. Open up to them let them know how you're feeling. Let them know what's bothering you and offer the same back to them.

Daring Movement: Self-Evaluation

> **Deep question time:**

Are you happy or unhappy?

What makes you happy?

Are there any areas in your life where you feel out of control?

Is it easier for you to do things for others than for yourself?

Does being around people energise you or not?

Do you like being in the spotlight?

How do you recharge?

What is your biggest day-to-day challenge?

Where do you find purpose in your life?

What upsets you?

What do you like to do after a bad day?

Who do you reach out to when you're sad?

I Can't do This Anymore

There's nothing weak about asking for help. It's actually the bravest thing you can do.

Daring Movement: A Loving Profile

Complete the sentence:

I love _____ about myself.

I wish I could:

My favourite feature about myself is:

What I love about my life:

What I don't love about my life:

I could make my life better by:

I really want:

List one thing you can do right now to make your day more ideal:

I want to feel:

I Can't do This Anymore

Hey, you. You don't have to do this alone. Use that powerful voice of yours to seek help.

A love letter to my teenage self
by Denise Frekling

> Denise is an editor with a passion for the written word. For as long as she remembers she's always had a book in her hands. You can find out more about her at Serious Moonlight Editing.

To Denise,

Buckle up, girl, because you're in for a helluva ride.

I get it. There's a lot of **pressure** in high school, and you've always had a flair for the dramatic (spoiler alert: that doesn't change as you get older), but I promise you that these things that are worrying you now are not the end of the world.

Not everyone is going to like you. You have what your mother lovingly refers to as a **strong** personality. Keep standing up for what you believe in and sharing opinions in class. Those people who pick on you are blinded by self-doubt and insecurity. It's not about you, not really. People can only like you to the degree in which they like themselves.

Not every **friendship** is going to last. It's okay to be sad that friendships don't last, but those memories you guys made together will last a lifetime (and so will those Polaroids). And who knows? Maybe one day you'll **reconnect** with childhood friends and forge a new, adult friendship.

Not every crush will reciprocate your **feelings**. In fact, you're going to get your **heart** broken several times. It's okay to cry about it but learn from it too. Even though it feels like the end of the world, and you're wondering how you're ever going to like someone else, let alone **love** someone else, ever again—you will. One day you're going to meet the most **amazing** person in the most unsuspected place, and you're going to pause for a single **breath** before jumping all-in.

Always be kind. The world doesn't have enough **kindness** in it, and you have plenty to share.

I don't want to go the way of many and say, "it gets better (when you get older)," because I like to think that it's not better or worse, it's just part of life. Part of your life. Your life is exactly as it should be, and it's a **fantastic** one.

Love,
Your older self x

Use Your Voice

Let's be who we really are.

Stand up for what you believe in. Stand up for what you don't agree with.

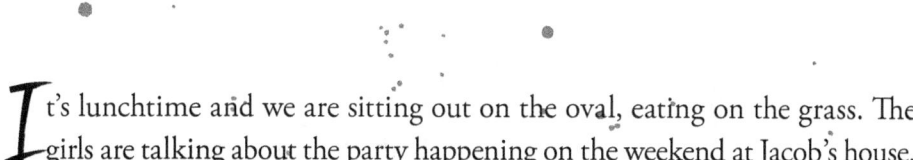

It's lunchtime and we are sitting out on the oval, eating on the grass. The girls are talking about the party happening on the weekend at Jacob's house.

"You still coming, Aimee?" Rachael asks, flicking her perfect straight blond hair over her shoulder.

I nod, chewing my shitty ham sandwich.

"Awesome. We'll get ready at my place after school on Friday. Just tell your parents you're crashing at mine," Rachael says.

"Yeah, sounds good." I smile, trying not to show the girls how nervous I am.

I just hope my parents will believe my lie. I'm not allowed to go to parties. They think that I'm too young. I'm sixteen and I beg to differ.

"Who's getting our drinks?" Amber asks, eyeballing Rachael. She has the connections in that department. Sammie laughs.

"Actually, Amber, my older bro is getting them for us," Sammie says.

She turns her back on Amber and whispers something to Rachael. They both laugh, throwing back their heads.

I sit quietly, watching the girls' interaction. Amber tries to hide her embarrassment with her long hair covering her face but I catch her bright red cheeks. She didn't mean to get it wrong, and the girls shouldn't be trying to isolate her.

The bell rings and the girls get up, brushing the grass off their butts. Sammie and Rachael start walking off, their arms hooked together. Amber and I follow close behind them. Sammie looks over her shoulder towards us.

"Maybe you shouldn't come on the weekend, Amber. My brother can't get you drinks anyway," Sammie says, then they both walk off.

I look over and see Amber's eyes start to water. I go to say something but before I get the chance she runs off, going straight for the girls' bathroom. I take a step to follow her.

"You coming, Aimee? We have PE together," Rachael yells.

I stay there for a moment, unsure of what to do. I rub the back of my neck. I want to go after Amber to make sure she's okay, but then the girls would kick me out too. I let out a sigh. Taking one last look towards the toilet, I turn away and catch up with the girls.

"She's such a loser. I don't even know why we hang out with her. Do you?" Rachael asks, staring right at me.

I don't know where to look now that both of the girls' attention is on me. Amber doesn't deserve to be talked about like this but what if the girls do this to me next? I wouldn't have anyone to hang around with. I wouldn't get invited to the cool parties. If you don't go with them, you aren't in, and being popular is everything.

I flick back my hair, just like Rachael did earlier.

"Yeah, total loser," I say, then laugh. The words feel like venom coming out of my mouth, but I have to say something. The girls look at each other and start laughing.

"See? We knew you'd agree." Sammie smirks.

I plaster a smile on my face to hide what I'm really feeling. I feel terrible saying those words, but I just have to remember why I need to.

The rest of the day flies by while I'm trying to play it cool with the girls. I don't see Amber in any of my classes and I'm starting to worry about her.

After walking into my house, I kick off my shoes and meet my mother in the kitchen.

"How was school, sweetie?" she asks, looking up from the papers scattered over the entire kitchen table.

I grab some grapes out of the fridge before placing them on the bench. Popping a grape into my mouth, I shrug. "Meh, it was okay."

"Don't sound too excited about it."

"Hey, Mum, can I stay at Rachael's on Friday night?" I ask, but I don't dare look up from the bag of grapes. Lying to my parents doesn't come easily. If I make eye contact, she'll see right through me straightaway.

It's silent for a good minute before I glance towards her. She's looking straight at me, her brows drawn together.

"Hmm, let me check with your father tonight." She pauses, moving her glasses down her nose. "What did you girls have planned?"

I freeze. Shit, I haven't come up with that lie yet. I suddenly feel hot. I clench my fists together. "Just hangin' out," I mutter, walking towards my room. *Abort, abort.*

Thankfully, I make it out of there into the safety of my room before she can drill me any further. Closing my door, I lean back against it and let out a sigh of relief.

My room's like any teenager's; my queen bed is covered in clothes I forgot to put away this morning. My walls are painted a pale blue that I'm totally in love with. Something about the colour calms me. After making my way over to my wooden desk, I pull out my journal and a pen. For the next hour, I write out what happened today and how I feel.

Dear Diary,

Today was terrible. The girls were really mean to Amber, and I didn't like it. I felt for Amber but what could I do about it? If I stood up for her, I'd be hated too. Being liked is everything, isn't it? I'd be alone if I said something, wouldn't I? High school is so confusing and hard. But I'm trying my best to be okay. I'm trying so hard to be this person that I'm not, just so I can be cool. But, Diary, it's hard being someone you aren't.

Yours, Aimee x

Friday comes around quickly. We are walking out of school on our way to Rachael's house. Rachael and Sammie are talking shit about Amber who I haven't seen all week. I tried to call her, but her mother said she's sick. Something doesn't feel right; I don't believe that she's really ill. I should go see her on Sunday and make sure she's okay. But right now, I have to focus on the party tonight. This is my chance to really fit in.

My party-attending record isn't too great because I hate lying to my parents, telling them I'll be somewhere that I'm not. But I have to suck it up. I need to prove that I can go out, get drunk, and party. My friends lie to their parents all the time. If they can do it, so can I. Although, Rachael's parents are totally cool with her drinking; that's why we're getting ready at her place. They are always out anyway and don't care what she does, which I'm totally jealous of. I wish my parents were like that. It would make everything so much easier.

We make it to Rachael's house after a short walk from school. Sammie's brother, Drew, meets us there at five o'clock, bringing us drinks. He's nineteen and says he will see us at Jacob's later on. Before he leaves, he looks me up and down then winks at me. My cheeks warm but I don't like the way he's staring at me like he wants to eat me.

"Ooh, Aimee is so into your brother, Sammie," Rachael teases as she slaps me playfully on the back.

I nervously look over to Sammie, waiting for her disapproval. She surprises me when she laughs.

"You can go for it, Aimee, but I don't think you're his type." Sammie pauses, looking me up and down.

I avoid her gaze; I don't like the way her eyes analyse my body.

"He has better taste," she snickers.

Ouch, that hurt.

She shares a look with Rachael. They both laugh but I don't think it's funny. *Aren't I pretty enough?*

Rachael puts our drinks in the fridge. I make my way over and take one. I need something to ease the embarrassment. Screwing the lid off the deep red Vodka soda, I swallow half of it down before coming up for a breath. Both the girls clap, encouraging me.

"Far out, Aimee. Who knew you could drink so well?" Rachael grins.

I smile, loving the little buzz that is forming within. This will help me tonight, so I can be myself at this party. Being around too many people makes me go back into my shell. Alcohol helps me be who I really am. Like I've dropped my mask.

We get ready while drinking. I've now had four drinks. I feel amazing; my confidence has skyrocketed.

We walk the short distance to Jacob's house and as we reach his block, you can hear the music pumping. My eyes light up as we walk down his driveway. There are people everywhere: on the front lawn and all the way down the side of his house into his backyard. They are all spread out in their little groups, laughing, talking, and drinking. I adjust my mini skirt, trying to pull it down.

Sammie grabs my hand, shaking her head. "Stop touching it. You won't make it look any better."

I cast my eyes down and swallow hard. She's right; I'll never pull this off.

We step into Jacob's backyard. Some people look our way as we enter but most don't even notice until Rachael squeals as Jacob grabs her around the waist and twirls her round. He places her back down and she swats him playfully.

"Where are the drinks at?" Sammie pipes up next to me.

"Inside, of course. You look like you could use another one, Aimee?" Drew appears next to Jacob, and he holds out his hand towards me.

My cheeks instantly heat. I hold the edge of my skirt nervously. Sammie lets out a loud laugh and walks off with Rachael and Jacob. I'm left with Drew who still has his hand outstretched, waiting for me.

"Come on, Aimee. I don't bite—*hard*." He winks.

A feeling of uneasiness settles over me. The way his eyes cast over me over creeps me out. But he's Sammie's brother and I can't shut him down.

Against my better judgment, I place my hand in his and he leads me towards the house. We move up the steps; there are people crowded everywhere in the open living room and kitchen area. Drew pulls me towards the kitchen where the girls are laughing with a group of boys from school, some seniors. Drew lets go of my hand and he slaps Jacob on the shoulder. He leans in, whispering something in his ear. Jacob smirks and they both look towards me. I avert my gaze to the girls, not liking the attention. My head feels dizzy. I need some water. Sammie's tongue-tied with one of the seniors, looking like they need a bedroom. Where is Rachael? I try to find her, but I can't see her anywhere. *I want to go home.*

Drew comes up behind me. I glance over my shoulder to see he's brought me a blueberry Cruiser. I don't want another drink, so I find myself shaking my head. He rolls his eyes and brushes away my hair before whispering into my ear, "Come on, babe. You'll be much more fun if you have this. Please, for me?" he begs.

My belly flips. I take the drink he holds over my shoulder. Screwing off the lid, I bring it to my lips. Drew holds on to my shoulders and starts massaging them. My gaze meets Rachael's and she winks at me. I smile back before downing half of my drink in two gulps. A burp erupts out of my mouth and I cover my lips, giggling.

"God, you're gorgeous. Come with me. I want to show you something."

Drew takes hold of my arm, leading me away from the girls. I feel light-headed but I try to keep my feet moving with his. Everything starts to become a bit blurry and in the next moment, we aren't in the house anymore. Goose bumps spread across my arms. It's quiet out here, apart from the music in the distance. Drew still holds one hand and in my other, I have my drink.

We suddenly stop. I glance around but I'm met with nothing but darkness.

"Can we go back?" I slur, my words not coming out clearly.

Drew grabs a hold of my shoulders. He brings my drink to my lips. I oblige by swallowing the rest of it. He takes it away once I've finished. My legs start to sway and I feel off, like I'm not in charge of my body anymore.

"Be a good little girl and lie on your back," Drew says from somewhere in front of me.

Unease fills me. I shake my head and start to move back. I don't want to do this. I want to go home.

Drew's hands roughly grab a hold of my shoulders. He pushes me and I'm falling backwards until the ground is beneath me.

"I don't want to," I slur, trying to lift myself back up.

But Drew's weight holds me down. He leans his body against my stomach, his size making it impossible to move.

"Please," I scream, trying to shake him off.

He laughs before he leans down, his breath against my ear. "You want this, Aimee. All the girls want this." His words confuse me. *Do all the girls really want this?*

My body gives up and I let him take control. Ugh, he keeps asking. I have to lose it sometime. I did want to be popular but is this the only way to do it? By letting him do what he wants with me? Tears spill down my cheeks. I'm so confused, I can't think straight. Maybe I'll just give up. It's easier than arguing.

He roughly grinds into me, rubbing his hardness against me. It doesn't feel good at all. It hurts. He takes my hands, pushing them above my head. His fingertips dig into my skin and I cry out.

"Shut the fuck up," he growls, tightening his grip on my hands.

He moves one hand down my stomach to my underwear. His hand feels rough on my skin; it feels wrong. He gathers up my skirt, pulling it up. Now my undies are exposed. He yanks them down and I shiver. His hand forcefully grabs my privates.

He digs his fingertips into my wrists. I think I see someone behind him, but it's hard to see in the dark. All I can make out is a dull light that's pointed at us.

"Cops, cops are here," a voice yells. The light vanishes and I hear whoever it was run away.

Drew jumps off me and disappears. I stay on the ground for a minute, trying to calm my beating heart. My head feels fuzzy and lost.

After a few minutes, I manage to pull up my undies and wiggle my mini skirt into place. I feel sick. I lean over, emptying my stomach that was full of nothing but alcohol. Once I finish, I wipe my mouth with the back of my hand. I stand and sway. Everything starts to spin. I look to what I think is the house to find everyone running in different directions. I need to find the girls and get out of here.

My body trembles as I walk the short distance back to the house. I find Rachael and Sammie by themselves out the back. Sammie looks me up and down then whispers something to Rachael. They both stare at me in disgust.

"Police. Stop where you are," an officer yells from somewhere to my right. The girls turn their backs and run in the opposite direction.

"Wait for me," I yell out to them, but they keep running.

I take a step and fall to my knees. Tears stream over my cheeks. I feel confused and have nowhere to go.

"You will need to come with us, miss." The officer appears in front of me, reaching out his hand. I take it and he lifts me up. *I'm going to be in serious trouble.*

He leads me to his car, and I give him my home address. As we drive off, I catch Sammie, Rachael, and Drew running out of the bushes. Drew has his arm around Rachael, and my stomach does backflips.

The officer in the driver's seat clears his throat. "Anything you want to tell me about tonight?"

I find myself instantly shaking my head. I can't tell them what happened with Drew. For one, they wouldn't believe me and I'd be in big trouble. Second, Drew would deny it and I'd be the laughingstock of school. It's not worth the drama that would follow.

I groan, rolling over as my phone buzzes on my bedside table. *What the hell?* I sit up and wish I hadn't. My head spins. It takes me a moment to regain my strength. I don't remember anything after I got into the cop car last night. But now I'm in my bed and my phone's going crazy with notifications. *What's going on?*

I reach over and open it. There are a million messages from the girls.

Sammie - You dirty hoe. Don't ever come to my house again. You aren't welcome.
Rachael - You and Drew? Wow, didn't think you had it in you.
Drew - You tell anyone, and they will be your last words. Keep ya mouth shut.

The colour drains from my face. How the hell do they know what happened with Drew? My finger clicks the Facebook app and I have more than one hundred notifications. Some guy from school, Andrew, has tagged me in a video. My stomach drops as I click it. It's of me and Drew last night. I grab my pillow and scream into it. Everyone has seen this. Me on my back with Drew over me. Everyone thinks that I'm a slut. My life is over.

Daring Support

If you too are struggling with what Aimee has gone through please seek professional help as soon as possible, you don't have to go through this by yourself. If someone forces themselves on you without your consent, it's not okay. You can report this and legal action will be taken against them. There are support systems out there that can listen, support and offer professional advice.
Please refer to page 261 for more information.

Confidence check-in

If we can take something from Aimee's story, it's learning to say no with confidence. We have all been there. We've found ourselves in situations where we think that we can't say no, that we have to go ahead. But that's far from the truth. We all have our own voice and we can use it to get out of situations that we aren't comfortable with.

On the next page are some examples of how Aimee could have used her voice to keep her out of harm's way.

Daring Culture: Staying Safe

> How can we do this? Let's take an example from Aimee's story:

"Come on, Aimee. I don't bite—hard." He winks.

A feeling of uneasiness settles over me. The way his eyes look me over creeps me out. But he's Sammie's brother and I can't shut him down.

Against my better judgment, I place my hand in his and he leads me towards the house.

> You *can* shut him down. You have your own voice. If you're feeling at unease, you don't have to go ahead with the situation. Aimee could have done this:

I take a step back, placing my hand on my hip.

"That's okay. I'm not feeling very well, and my parents are about to pick me up."

Drew shrugs and walks off.

> See how easy that is? She let Drew know she wasn't in the mood to party with him and she made clear there were people who were expecting to meet her shortly. Now Aimee can be safe and not feel trapped by thinking that she doesn't have a choice. We always have a choice in every situation.

Daring Culture: Saying NO

Different ways to say no:

- No thanks. I have a family thing.
- I wish I could make it work.
- I wish, but my parents won't let me go out this weekend.
- Sounds great, but sorry I can't commit.
- There's so much going on at home.
- I'd love to, but I can't.
- I've orgainised to meet a friend at XX o'clock, so I really can't leave.
- I just see you as a friend.
- I'm seeing someone else.

Use Your Voice

What is strength?

Strength is not hurting those who hurt you. Strength is turning your back on someone that doesn't treat you well. Strength is being able to smile even when everything feels like it's falling apart. Strength is you.

Daring Movement: Breathing Meditation

> You may get into a situation that makes you uncomfortable. Your heart starts beating faster and faster until you can't take it anymore. Here is a simple meditation you can do that can help with bringing you back to a calm place.

Find a quiet place, for example, go to the bathroom and close the door. Shut your eyes and take a deep breath in. Open your mouth and let it out. Take another deep breath, hold, and let it all out. Focus on nothing except for your breath. Imagine it filling every part of you, all the way to your toes. Continue to do this until the weight has been lifted off your shoulders.

> You can also do this without having to leave wherever you are, a friend's place or a party.

Use Your Voice

Daring Culture: Owning You

> **What does being 'cool' mean to you?**

Is it following the popular girl in school and doing everything that she is doing?

Would you prefer to be exactly who you are and rise on your own two feet? To stand up for what you don't like or agree with and make your own decisions, not following or doing what anyone else is?

To me, being cool is listening to my own thoughts and doing exactly what I want. It's being true to yourself and everyone around you. We have too many followers in the world. Let's be who we really are.

Is it really everything to be invited to these parties?

I used to believe that it was. That if I didn't go, I would miss out on everything and it would be the end of the world. But honestly, it's not worth the headache and drama that follows the next day. You attend the party, drink, and be someone who you are not. I'm not saying that you shouldn't go to parties if that's what you want to do. But I'm saying you have a choice.

- ♥ *Go if you want to.*
- ♥ *Don't go* just to be seen as a 'cool' person.

> Have your own voice and make your own decisions based on what YOU want to do.

Daring Movement: This or That

Tick which you would rather do.

THIS	THAT
☐ Be yourself	☐ Be someone you're not
☐ Follow your friend	☐ Turn your back on your friend
☐ Stand up for what matters	☐ Have no voice
☐ Be comfortable in your own skin	☐ Be uncomfortable in your own skin
☐ Walk with confidence	☐ Hide behind a mask
☐ Face your fears	☐ Forget you have them
☐ Be safe because you said no	☐ Be in a bad situation

Use Your Voice

Your wings may be broken but they will always heal and become stronger.

Daring Movement: Priorities

Let's get our priorities sorted. Create a chart of how your time is currently balanced with your priorities. For example: family, friends, study, work, exercise.

How I currently spend my time.

How I want to spend my time.

Use Your Voice

Don't be well known; be worth knowing.

Don't be well known; be worth knowing.

Daring Movement: Priorities

Let's get our priorities sorted. Create a chart of how your time is currently balanced with your priorities. For example: family, friends, study, work, exercise.

How I currently spend my time.

How I want to spend my time.

Use Your Voice

Daring Culture: Stand Up

Aimee didn't like the way her friends were treating Amber. But she didn't say anything, afraid that they would turn on her. I know I've been in this situation too and it's a hard one. An important thing to remember here is that we should *always* stand up for what we don't agree with. Otherwise, we will go through our life always saying yes and going along with things that we really don't want to be a part of. You can shape your destiny.

Daring Movement: Mantras

> Write down some mantras that you want to remind yourself of every day.

Daring Culture: Looking Out For Friends

> Follow your friend and make sure she's okay.
> That's what good friends do.

Let's put ourselves in Aimee's shoes for a second. Would you want your friends to follow after you to make sure you were okay? I know I would and if my 'friends' didn't, then I'd know they weren't true friends.

How can we do this? Let's take an example from Aimee's story:

> "She's such a loser. I don't even know why we hang out with her. Do you?" Rachael asks, staring right at me. I don't know where to look now that both of the girls' attention is on me. Amber doesn't deserve to be talked about like this but what if the girls do this to me next? I wouldn't have anyone to hang around with. I wouldn't get invited to the cool parties. If you don't go with them, you aren't in, and being popular is everything.
>
> I flick back my hair just like Rachael did earlier.
>
> "Yeah, total loser." I laugh. The words feel like venom coming out of my mouth, but I have to say something.

Aimee could have done this:

> "Yeah I do, because she is our friend and I should go check on her to make sure she's okay."

Such a simple and easy response, but it's an easy way to stick up for your friend in a subtle way. It's also a little reminder to Rachael that she is their friend and that's why they hang out with her.

Daring Movement: Questions To Ask Your Friends

Questions to ask a friend in need.

- Are you okay? Like really okay?
- What happened today really sucks. Want to talk about it?

Come up with your own questions to ask a friend in need.

We don't lose friends.
We find out who
our real friends are
when we become
our true self.

A love letter to my teenage self
by Jenna Black

> Jenna is a spiritual abundance queen and manifestation expert. You can find out more about her here www.abundantboss.com

Dear Jenna,

I know you feel completely lost and stuck right now. It's as if nobody hears you, or really sees you. As much as you try, you just don't fit in. **Beautiful** girl, I want you to know this: that sweet, **sensitive** heart of yours might feel like it hurts too often, but really, it's your greatest superpower.

That **intuitive** soul of yours might feel overwhelming at times, but really, it's your inner GPS—please trust it.

That **creative** mind of yours, which is constantly daydreaming in class, may get you in trouble sometimes, but really, it's your tool for manifesting your wildest desires.

Those stretch marks on your body may feel uncomfortable, but really, they are lightning bolts of growth and **power**.

Those green wild eyes of yours may cry tears of sadness and frustration, but they are **destined** to see so much **magic** and love in your future.

Beautiful girl, right now you are **hurting**. You're caught up in the wrong crowd, changing who you are on the outside to 'fit in' and finally feel accepted. The drinking, the partying, the rebellious attitude—deep down, it's not really you. And it pains you to put on this mask, cover up your true self, and be someone you're not.

I know it feels like your worth is defined by your inner circle, what crowd you're accepted into, and how wild and rebellious you can 'prove' yourself to be. But I also see you hurting, my love. Because you are **seeking** your worth outside of yourself, and it's a vicious cycle that never seems to end.

Constantly seeking approval from your friends.
Constantly putting on a mask.
Constantly wanting to feel accepted while hiding the real you.
It's tiring, isn't it?

Beautiful girl, I want you to know this: nobody can define your worth. You are **divinely worthy** as you are. And that validation you are seeking? It comes from within you.

Your older self x

The Inner Critic

Your mind is one of the most powerful tools you have. Treat it with kindness.

My head is down as I walk into school—like it is every morning when I drag myself to this hell. My eyes are downcast, my hair falls over my face, and I don't want anyone to notice me. If they do, I know what they will think.

Opening the door to my locker, I glance up for a split second and that's my first mistake. Ally and her friends are gathered around their lockers. Ally looks me up and down, but I don't dare maintain eye contact.

I know what she'll be thinking: *Look at her. She's pathetic, a fat pig who doesn't deserve to be here.* My chest starts to ache, and I feel sick. She's right; I am all those things and much more.

After throwing my bag into my locker, I spin around, walking as fast as I can straight to the bathroom. I manage to pull my hair back just in time as I empty my guts into the toilet. Sweat trickles down my forehead. I sit back on my heels, wiping my lips with the sleeve of my school jumper. My temperature starts to cool down, but my heart still feels like it's going a million miles. Clutching my stomach, I wonder why I can't be like Ally. Everyone thinks I'm disgusting, not even worth looking at. The bell rings through the bathroom. I will my body to move but I don't want to go out there. Out there means judgment.

The sound of the bathroom door opening and swinging shut pulls me straight up. I brush down my clothes, taking a deep breath before I leave the safety of the cubical where there's only judgement from myself.

I make it into my classroom without running into anyone. I sit down in the back of the class, right in the far corner so I have eyes on everyone else and they don't have eyes on me. The room starts to fill, chatter floods my ears, and my palms begin to sweat. I keep my eyes down while I fiddle with my notebook, trying not to draw attention to myself.

Problem is, when I'm around others, I don't know how to act. How to move, how to talk properly, how to walk normally without bringing attention to myself. How to be cool and natural. Every movement I make is well-thought-out before it happens. I have to do this—otherwise, I'll draw unwanted attention to myself and they will start calling me names. I want to be like Ally and her friends; they know how to be themselves naturally. Every time they move, people look at them in awe. I see it in their eyes. I want people to look at me like that. But no one ever does. I am an outcast, a worthless human being, a weirdo. I'm sure they all think that of me. That's why no one ever comes near me, like I am invisible. But I like that. It means they can't tell me what they think of me out loud.

As soon as the bell rings for lunch, everyone quickly walks out of the classroom. I'm last to leave; only the teacher remains.

"Are you okay, Rebecca?" Mrs Samuels asks from her desk as I walk to the door.

I manage to nod before reaching the exit. I need air. I need to breathe.

"It's okay to talk. I'm always here," she offers, but I know she doesn't mean it.

Does she even care? My mind's screaming at me, telling me that she doesn't care one bit. But there's a small part of me that wonders if she might. I quickly shut down that part of me and leave in a hurry.

Great, the worst part of my day. I enter the playground, it's like a zoo around here. Everyone has their group that they sit with. They belong, they know their friends, and who they share interests with.

Me? I don't belong anywhere. I'm an outcast who nobody wants in their clique. I grab my sandwich from my locker before making my way to my one safe place: the library. There I can hide from prying eyes.

On my way to the library, I hear someone yell out my name.

My body freezes and I panic, keeping my eyes on the footpath. My breathing becomes shallow, my foot gets caught on something, and I trip. My body lands hard against the pavement. *Ow.* My teeth grit together, and I curse under my

breath. I quickly glance around, praying that no one saw what happened. They will all be laughing at me right now. I catch someone coming my way, then they are there right in front of me.

"Oh my God. Are you okay, Rebecca?" It's Ally. She places her hand on my elbow, helping me off the ground.

My knees are bleeding from the gravel rash, but I don't care about that. Everyone's looking at me now. Ally thinks I'm a complete loser who can't walk. I can't bear to see the pity in her eyes.

I do the one and only thing I know how to: I run.

Straight into the library and away from everyone.

The rest of the day, I keep my head down and don't interact with anyone. Ally tries to talk to me, but I can't give her anything back. She just sees me as this complete idiot who can't look after herself. She doesn't really want to be nice; there's got to be a reason behind it.

My mother picks me up from school and at home, I lock myself away in my bedroom. My journal is laid out in front of me, the blank page staring back at me, begging for words. For the first time today, I smile and put my pen to the paper.

Dear Diary,

I'm trying my best to be okay, but I'm really not. I don't know how to act in front of others. I feel lost, Diary. How can I be me when I hate myself that much? Nobody but you would understand how it feels when I walk into a room. I see them looking right through me. I hear exactly what they are thinking. I know everyone believes I'm a complete loser who's got no friends. How do I change that, Diary? How do I turn all these negative voices into positive ones? Will I ever have friends? Will I ever be able to let anyone in enough to create that bond that I so desperately crave? Or will I be like this forever? Please help me, Diary, because I'm lost and I can't find my way back.

Rebecca

Daring Support

If you too are struggling with what Rebecca has gone through please seek professional help as soon as possible, you don't have to go through this by yourself. There are support systems out there that can listen, support and offer professional advice.
Please refer to page 261 for more information.

Inner Critic check-In

We all have an inner critic—the one who's always putting us down. I like to call her my evil stepsister. She's our worst critic. She's always analysing every situation and telling us things that bring us down. Without realising it, you can put up a wall around us that blocks everyone else out. It's a barrier that makes people second-guess talking to you. Because you don't look approachable—perhaps you don't look like you want to be talked to or loved. Really, that's exactly what you are craving. It takes some practice, but you can quiet down that voice until she's filled with love and kindness. You can take those walls down.

Daring Culture: The Inner Critic

One way you can help quiet your inner bitch (yep, that's her name now) is to switch everything she says. **For example:**

I am pathetic > I am worthwhile.

See how easy that was? Now let's really put this to action.

She will think that I'm a complete loser > She's coming to help me; that means she must care.

I am an outcast > I deserve to have friends.

I am worthless > I am worth it.

You deserve to give yourself the love that you give out.

We spend too much of our lives worrying about how we act, talk, and walk. It can become quite exhausting and it's entirely unnecessary. We shouldn't be worrying about how we act; we are all unique and should be free to behave naturally. Not how we *should*. Do you really want to be someone that you are not, just to fit in and be like everyone else?

I don't, I want to be myself. To walk with my head held high and make decisions that I choose. Not be influenced into making them based on what I believe people will think. Because nine times out of ten, others aren't even aware of you and what you're doing. We're all too wrapped up in our own stuff to notice! Everyone is the same.

Daring Movement: Taming your Inner Critic

Now it's your turn.

I am a loser >

They will all laugh at me >

She thinks that I'm a mess >

Nobody even notices me >

She thinks I'm ugly >

Tell your inner critic to sit down and *shut up.*

Daring Culture: Missing Out

Let's take a look at this part of Rebecca's story, for example:

My body lands hard against the pavement. Ow. My teeth grit together, and I curse under my breath. I quickly glance around, praying that no one saw what happened. They will all be laughing at me right now. I catch someone coming my way, then they are there right in front of me.

"Oh my God. Are you okay, Rebecca?" It's Ally. She places her hand on my elbow, helping me off the ground.

My knees are bleeding from the gravel rash, but I don't care about that. Everyone's looking at me now. Ally thinks I'm a complete loser who can't walk. I can't bear to see the pity in her eyes.

I do the one and only thing I know how to: I run.

Straight into the library and away from everyone.

Ally actually wants to help Rebecca and doesn't think that she's a loser. Rebecca is thinking the worst and making up stories in her head that aren't the truth. If Rebecca opened up to Ally and thanked her for helping, there could be a beautiful friendship to form and Rebecca wouldn't be alone anymore.

We need to open up to those around us. Let others use their own voices to tell us how they see us instead of the ones that we project on to them.

Don't close yourself off, my darling. You have so much to offer the world.

Daring Culture: What's Normal?

> Remember how Rebecca felt when she was at school?

Problem is, when I'm around others, I don't know how to act. How to move, how to talk properly, how to walk normally without bringing attention to myself. How to be cool and natural. Every movement I make is well-thought-out before it happens. I have to do this—otherwise, I'll draw unwanted attention to myself and they will start calling me names. I want to be like Ally and her friends; they know how to be themselves naturally. Every time they move, people look at them in awe. I see it in their eyes. I want people to look at me like that. But no one ever does. I am an outcast, a worthless human being, a weirdo. I'm sure they all think that of me.

> Rebecca *does* know how to act, how to move, how to talk properly, and how to walk normally. She is just like everyone else around her apart from one thing: her inner critic. *She* tells her that she's different.
>
> Who made a rule book saying we should walk, talk, act, and dress a certain way? Nobody did or will because every one of us is different and that's so beautiful. Rebecca needs a gentle reminder of this—that there is no right or wrong way to do things. That she should just be herself and stop worrying so much. Once she does this, she will be surprised by how many people she attracts. People won't be afraid to talk to her because her protective wall will be down.

The Inner Critic

One of the most courageous things to do is to apologise to yourself for the nasty words and heartache you have caused.

Daring Movement: Word Search

Self-care – the first three words you see is what you need right now

A	R	G	B	A	T	H	M	T
M	E	D	I	A	T	I	O	N
N	E	T	F	L	I	X	T	I
G	X	Q	P	W	A	L	K	O
C	H	O	C	O	L	A	T	E
D	A	B	O	O	K	V	Z	P
A	F	R	I	E	N	D	T	Y
N	A	T	U	R	E	V	U	H
G	A	Q	M	B	E	A	C	H
C	R	Y	S	T	A	L	S	M
T	A	H	U	G	S	H	T	K
S	V	M	R	E	S	T	B	E
K	L	A	U	G	H	T	E	R
M	T	F	A	M	I	L	Y	P

The Inner Critic

Journal Writing check-in

Have you ever tried journal writing? Or you may be thinking 'what actually is journal writing' and that's okay. Journaling is for anyone who benefits from writing it all out and letting go of all your thoughts on paper. It's quite a healing process that can help clear that busy mind of yours.

You can jot down things that you may be thinking about, random questions, or you may actually like to draw out what's on your mind. The aim is to get your emotions and thoughts out of your head (and heart) and perhaps allow you to look at them and evaluate from another perspective. You don't have to keep everything all bottled up inside; journaling can be a release.

There are a few different kinds of journaling you can do. You can simply finish your day off by writing down what happened, what you're feeling, or what you want to resolve. Or you can start the day with a moment of journaling, setting up affirmations on how you want your day to be, and how you want to feel. There is no right or wrong way to do it. This is for you only, so have some fun, experiment with new techniques, and find what works best for you. Remember Rebecca's diary entry at the end of her rough day? That's a great example of how powerful journal writing can be. It helped Rebecca clear the thoughts from her mind.

Dear Diary,

I'm trying my best to be okay, but I'm really not. I don't know how to act in front of others. I feel lost, Diary. How can I be me when I hate myself that much? Nobody but you would understand how it feels when I walk into a room.

I see them looking right through me. I hear exactly what they are thinking. I know everyone believes I'm a complete loser who's got no friends. How do I change that, Diary? How do I turn all these negative voices into positive ones? Will I ever have friends? Will I ever be able to let anyone in enough to create that bond that I so desperately crave? Or will I be like this forever? Please help me, Diary, because I'm lost and I can't find my way back.

Rebecca

> See how powerful journal writing is? It helped Rebecca clear those thoughts from her mind. It's a step in the right direction.

Daring Culture: Journal Prompts

> Here are some prompts to get you started. Remember, a blank page is full of possibilities.

Today I learnt ...
Today was bad because ...
I am ...
My ideal day looks like ...
In my life, I need more ...
Ten things I love about myself and why ...
If someone else described me they would say ...
The person I look up to the most is and the reasons why are ...

One of the best ways we can heal is from the inside out.

Daring Movement: Journaling

> Come up with your own journal prompts.
> I've started you off with a couple more.

Today will be ...

I'm struggling with ...

The Inner Critic

Daring Movement: Dear Inner Critic

> Write a love letter to your inner critic. Stick up for yourself. Tell her all the reasons you're actually doing okay.

Dear ...

Do your thing, you are a limited edition.

A love letter to my teenage self
by Shannon Wills

> Shannon is a natural skin care specialist who makes her own products. You can find out more about her here www.simplicityaroma.com/

To Shannon,

Just breathe ...

Be **kinder** to yourself; you are exactly where and who you are meant to be.

Your **compassion** and empathy is raw and real and teaching you valuable lessons that will give you the **strength** you need to fulfill your dreams.

Be gentle with yourself and your thoughts. You already know the things that light you up so stop judging and letting self-doubt creep in. **You are not lost** and were never made to follow the leader, so don't try to compare yourself to others. You have your own path.

Your **determination**, when you set your mind to something is unstoppable. You can be headstrong and fierce, and you have the most amazing female role models in your life to question and drive you if and when you need it, so stop getting in your own way.

You are surrounded by a group of incredible friends who you'll grow up to appreciate more than ever. And the unconditional love you have and receive from them and your family will be the strength you need to truly **follow your heart**.

So **just breathe** and be kinder with your words and thoughts to yourself. Trust your instincts and know how loved and supported you are. You've got this.

Love your older self x

Can't You Understand

Let's stand together as one.

Written by Amara Kent

I still haven't made any friends, so finding a spot to have lunch is difficult. The cafeteria is busy, and there is hardly a place for someone like me. If I manage to get there early enough, I am able to secure a spot, whilst other times I go and eat my lunch in the toilet. Today I am lucky; I am lucky enough to get a spot at the back. Away from people. Nobody will bug me, because nobody wants to speak to the loser foreign student with broken English.

I had quickly shoved my books in my locker, grabbed my Kindle, and made my way to the cafeteria, I pick up a chicken schnitzel burger, a cola, and chips. I have somehow convinced my mother that being here, I should start to eat foods others won't find offensive as they aren't used to the smells we are accustomed to.

At first, she had refused, but eventually, she acquiesced, agreeing that it would probably be best, and I'm not exactly giving up my culture by assimilating. I am merely acclimatising to the life I am now resigned to living.

I haven't been seated for five minutes when the nasty girl decides she will sashay up to me. I don't know what she wants. She's refused to acknowledge my existence outside of the few classes we share together.

This doesn't bode well for me, I know it.

My gut tightens.

I glare past her to her table. The table that is reserved for them. They don't need to inform people. Everyone just knows.

She stops short, resting her hands on my table, her breasts protruding thanks to the support of her push-up bra. They were straining against the confines of her sports uniform. She gazes at me with a sparkle in her eyes. A sparkle that is there whenever she is about to pummel someone to the ground after ripping their heart out.

I remove my focus from her, pulling my head down and concentrating on my lunch in front of me, picking at my chips.

"I'm so sorry about my behaviour in English. I've been advised that I need to be a little more compassionate towards those who struggle with English. By way of apology, I would like to extend an invitation to sit with me and my friends."

There is nothing innocent about this interaction.

She hasn't even attempted to hide her miscreant intent.

I'm not falling for it though. I know what could happen. Contrary to popular opinion, I'm not stupid.

I politely decline with a shake of my head and instantly her sickly sugar-sweet smile turns into an angered frown.

Leaning in farther, she gets right in my face. "Listen here, you stupid bitch, I don't hand out these invitations to anyone, and despite my feelings towards you, it's been demanded that I be nicer to you. Just come sit with us so I can get the damn principal off my back."

"N-N-N-N-No," I stutter.

"Suit yourself. But let me tell you this, you ever squeal on me to the principal again, I will make your high school experience hell." And with that, and a quick flick of her perfectly done-up hair, she skips off, returning to her place in the middle of the cafeteria where everyone can see and admire her.

I don't know how much worse things can get for me. How much worse she can make it for me. I don't have any friends. Nobody wants a bar of the girl who they can't relate to or communicate with.

I haven't ratted her out to the principal. There is honour amongst good and the bad—at least when it comes to high school—you respect the honour code, and nothing bad can happen to you.

You respect the honour code, and you are left relatively alone.

She calculated one plus one and got apple, assuming I had been the one to want to go toe to toe with her by informing the principal. I'm not going to tell anyone that she's a bully. Ever. That is one thing I am certain of.

I am uncomfortable under her intense stare I can feel from all the way at the back of the cafeteria. I rush to finish my lunch, not caring about the possibility of indigestion. I gather my things and quickly walk past her table. But as I do, I trip, falling flat on my face.

The surprise introduction of my body to the hard timber floor is not welcome and a shock to my body. A sharp pain shoots straight through me.

I grit my teeth, a shrill sound escaping through my teeth.

The cafeteria erupts into laughter. Guffaws ring loudly in my ears as I hang my head.

I want to get out of there.

Need to get out of there.

I quickly rush up, but my swift escape is stopped short by the perpetrator and her friends.

They circle around me, glaring at me and flashing taunting and malicious smirks. The nasty girl is in front of me, and I am eye level with her, unable to escape her targeted stare.

With one blink, she pushes me into the hands of somebody else, who then pushes me against somebody else. From there, I am used like a ball—much like the one you would find in a pinball machine. They are shouting things at me and laughing, clapping with glee as they toss me around their little circle of friends before they push me straight back on the ground. I slide along a little way, my things spreading across the ground. The noise excruciatingly as the rest of the school choruses their enjoyment at seeing me suffer.

"Ooh, walk much, bitch? You need to be careful when you walk. Watch where you're going!" The nasty girl's voice slams into me.

I want to grab my things and run, but their laughter is freezing me to the spot. I scurry back, trying to gain some distance between me and the popular group.

Without a word, the ringleader stretches her eyes out using her fingers—a ruthless imitation of my own.

And right then and there, I do the one thing I vowed I wouldn't do. I break down. The tears fall freely. All I can see now is a sea of students, as they copy what the nasty girl did.

I race to the place I should have gone to in the first place.

My sanctuary.

As disgusting as it is, it is the only place I can go and be left alone.

Tearing down the halls, the sounds become muffled then farther away. I fling open the door. It smacks against the tiled wall, and I lock myself into the last cubicle.

My body is wracked from the torture.

The hatred I feel for myself.

I can no longer hold myself strong.

I just want to leave this school. This world.

I'm hated because I look different.

Hated because I can't communicate in the free way they can.

Hated because sometimes I misunderstand what people say because I am still navigating my way through the language.

And right then and there, I feel the same hatred they do.

I hate myself for the way I look, and the country I was born in. I hate my mother because it is *her* fault that she allowed me to live. Knowing full well what I looked like, she was selfish in thinking that it was okay to bring me into this world.

Daring Support

If you too are struggling with what Elle has gone through please seek professional help as soon as possible, you don't have to go through this by yourself. There are support systems out there that can listen, support and offer professional advice.

Please refer to page 261 for more information.

Discrimination check-in

We shouldn't be judged by the colour of our skin. Instead, we should be treated equally, no matter what we look like, or how we act, speak, or walk. We are all unique and different and that's so beautiful.

Think back to the last time you made a friend. Did you observe her first before she opened her mouth? You probably did; we all do. But after that, we say hello and we talk before we decide if we can be friends or not. It doesn't matter how we look; we all have one thing in common: we are human beings who all equally deserve a chance.

We learn from each other. I have friends of all nationalities and it's so amazing learning about their heritage. Each nationality has its own unique foods which we may get to try when we go out for dinner at a restaurant.

> Would you want your friend to feel like this?

I look nothing like the students around me, thanks to my black almond-shaped eyes, my thick black hair cut to my shoulders, and my bangs that make me look like a doll and five years younger than I am. Together with my slim figure and naturally darker skin tone, I stand out like a lighthouse in a storm.

> If I knew my friend thought this about herself, it would make me really upset. Every single human being deserves to feel normal, no matter what they look like. It shouldn't matter what colour skin we have, or what features we have. What should matter is what's on the inside, and what kind of people we are to each other.

Let's make a difference with our differences.

I have learnt some important lessons since moving here:

A) People aren't as accepting towards non-English speaking foreigners as much as they proclaim themselves to be.

B) People are ignorant to think that if you don't speak their language, they can loudly and proudly talk about you without any consequence, and without you being able to decipher their obvious code.

> Do we want someone to feel like this? Or do we want to make a change and accept everyone, no matter their nationality?

Daring Culture: Standing Up

This is how you could respond to racist remarks made to yourself or if you overhear them directed at someone else.

> To stand up for yourself or your friend,
> you could say something like this:

"Why would you say that? It's really mean and unnecessary."

> Fight back with knowledge; this can educate the person.

"When you say that Asians are better at math, you're stereotyping a whole group of people, which isn't fair to them. Each person is unique; we shouldn't judge based on race."

Don't judge people. Learn from them.

Daring Culture: No Racism

> You can help by doing your part.

♥ **Report racism to a higher authority.**
Going to talk to the principal about something you have seen or experienced firsthand can help stop racism. Schools don't accept this behaviour and by telling someone higher up, you will contribute to stamping it out.

♥ **Ask your school to educate students about racism.**
If we are all educated about racism and know how this impacts us, our friends, and peers, we will remove it from schools for good.

♥ **Discover new cultures.**
The more we embrace the traditions, cuisine, and overall cultures of the people in our schools and community, the more we open ourselves up to equality and exciting new experiences.

A love letter to my teenage self
by Anja May

Anja is an author and owner of Mysterious Crates & Books. You can find out more about her here www.etsy.com/au/shop/MysteriousCrates

Dear Anja,

You have been so very **lonely**, trying to find a place you feel at home. You try to **escape** the life you've been handed, but darling, let me tell you it's not as bad as it feels. Only, you'll need to go through those hard times to see all this pain will be worth it. I just need you to know that no guy will ever fill that hole. You'll fall in and out of love. It will be beautiful and **heartbreaking**, but you will get through it.

You'll chase after friends and people you think are your ticket out of this hellhole of a town. The thing you don't know is they are just as lost as you are. The road you take isn't easy. I wish I could tell you the answer isn't getting high and forgetting your **problems**, and that going out and partying isn't how you get **real friends**. But the only way we seem to learn is by doing everything the hard way.

Your eating disorder has turned worse. You're now only 44kg. Your **anxiety** is at its peak and your **depression** at its lowest. You've locked yourself in your house, not able to leave, too terrified for anyone to see you and realise how much weight you have lost. No one can help because no one can **understand** what you're going through. You feel like you're drowning, unable to break the surface. Each time your fingers break through, you're pulled down deeper. This is your lowest point.

It's okay though. You pull yourself out of this. You have people around you, but you do it alone. You do all of it alone, but you have one person, and I wish I could tell you to lean on him the most. Your brother—no one, and I mean *no one* will understand you like he does. He's your rock and he has every intention of never leaving your side. He won't either. He has your back; he's the only male who would and always will flip the world just to help you. Never forget how much he loves you. He will always be there.

Life starts to get better after this. You will always struggle with these things but you're at peace with most of it now. You dress up, go out, and enjoy life more. You WILL get there, I promise, even if it doesn't feel like it. You are **beautiful**. You are strong. You can take on the world.

I've done it; I know. Now pick that good butt up and go conquer the world and let everyone see you shine!

Love from your older self x

Lift that head of yours, beautiful.

Show the world that you won't fall at their hands.

Think Before You Type

My phone dings from my bedside table. Absently, I reach for it before sliding it open. It takes a moment for my eyes to adjust. A million messages appear. I sit up in bed. My heart starts beating faster as I begin reading them.

Emma: What the hell were you thinking?
Ava: You're a piece of shit.
Mia: Don't ever talk to me again. You are done.
Derick: Meet me in the locker rooms. I'll show you a better time.

I feel sick. I quickly open the Facebook app and the first thing I see is the image. The colour drains from my face. It's of Ethan leaning into me, his lips touching mine. My stomach flips as the memories come flooding back. I throw my phone across my bed and run towards my bathroom. I make it just in time as I empty my stomach into the toilet. Wiping my mouth with the back of my hand, I sink into my heels. Tears fall down my cheeks. How could I have been so stupid? Memories come flooding back from that day in the locker room.

It was Friday afternoon and my phone buzzed in my pocket. I pulled it out sliding it open.

Ethan – Meet me in the boys' locker room after school.

I quickly responded while I walked down the corridor.

Me – Why?

Ethan – I want to talk with you about Mia. But don't tell the girls.

Mia was my best friend who happened to be dating Ethan. If he wanted to talk about her there must be something going on.

Me – Yep, see ya soon.

I caught the girls at my locker, after placing my books inside I said my goodbyes to my friends, Emma, Ava, and Mia, saying I had to go see Mr Haynes about gym class. The lie felt wrong, but Ethan said to not tell anyone about our meet up. That it had to be a secret. I never went behind my friends' backs, but he said it was important and it was about Mia, so I had to do it for her.

I waited outside the boys' locker room until everyone piled out. I stepped inside for the first time ever. It was much like the girls' one: rows of lockers that led into an open area with change tables and showers lining the wall. The room was empty and silent except for the dripping of the water.

"Hello, Ethan, you here?" I yelled out. My voice echoed off the walls, and I started to feel uneasy.

When no response came, I took a step backwards, then another. I spun around and ran straight into a solid chest. The air left my lungs and my heart started beating faster. My hands were on his bare chest. I quickly pulled back, looking up at a smirking Ethan.

"There you are. Been looking for you. Come on, let's talk back here." Ethan took my hand, and I followed him behind the lockers in the change room area. He placed his backpack on the table.

"What did you want to talk about? Is everything okay with Mia?" I asked, placing my arms over my ribs.

Ethan nodded and tapped his hand on the seat beside him. I walked over and sat, smoothing my skirt before turning to look at Ethan. He stared straight ahead without saying a word. The silence was deafening. I went to stand, but

Ethan's hand shot out, landing on my knee and holding me there.

"Are you going to tell me why you invited me here?" My patience was starting to wear thin. I had more important things to do than wait around for Ethan to speak.

"Charlotte, do you know what I like about you?" His voice sent a shiver down my spine.

I found myself shaking my head. His hand started moving farther up my leg. I pushed his hand away, but he quickly placed it back there before gripping my leg tight.

"That you don't realise how hot you are. You walk around in short skirts showing off your hot body, begging for it to be touched."

I gasped and stood up.

"What the hell, Ethan? You're in a relationship with my best friend. I'll do you a favour and forget you just said that. This never happened." I huffed and started walking away.

His hand flew out, grabbing my wrist. Pain shot up my arm as his grip tightened. His green eyes sparkled. I'd never seen this side of him before. He looked like he wanted to eat me alive. His tongue slid over his top lip as he looked me up and down. My stomach dropped; I didn't like the way he was staring at me. I wanted to get away from him; he was starting to freak me out. I tried to pull my arm free, but Ethan's grip was too tight.

"Let me go, Ethan," I growled.

He laughed and started to yank me towards the showers. I tried to scream for help. Ethan abruptly stopped. My back slammed against the brick wall. I whimpered as pain shot up my spine. He covered my mouth with his hand and my screams for help dulled.

He leaned down and whispered in my ear, "You want this, Char. I see the way you look at me. You've been begging for this."

I shook my head, unable to speak. He was lying. I never looked at him like that. I didn't want him and never would. He moved his hand away, then leaned in before smashing our lips together. I kept my mouth shut. My hands found his chest and I pushed hard. He fell back slightly, and that was all I needed.

I ran and I didn't look back.

A loud knock on my door breaks me from my memories.

"Sweetie, you're going to be late for school," my mother yells through my bedroom.

I quickly stand, trying to wipe away the tears. My legs give out and I fall back down. The ground bites against my skin. I hear the door to my room open but I can't move. My heart feels like it's broken into a million pieces. I can't go back to school. Everyone hates me. *I* hate me for letting Ethan touch me like that. Mia hates me and so do my other friends. My life is over.

My mother's gasp fills the room. My eyes meet hers and I don't need to say a word. She kneels down, taking me in her arms. My head falls against her chest. I stay there, filling my mother's chest with tears. She lets me fall apart and the best bit is, she doesn't ask me what's wrong.

I can't tell her what I've done. She won't like what happened, that I did this to my best friend. I pull back and wipe away the last of my tears.

"Want to talk about it?" she asks, giving me her hand. She helps me up.

I shake my head. "Just please don't make me go to school. I can't, Mum. I can't face them." My voice breaks and I'm about to lose it again when my mother's words stop me.

"Just today, sweetheart. You will have to face up to whatever this is about one day. I will give you today to rest and recover. I know you're not ready to tell me what happened. But I'm always here for you. I won't judge."

But she would. What happened isn't right. I stuffed up.

My mother sets me up in my bed, leaving some snacks, magazines, and movies to watch on my laptop. She kisses me goodbye and heads off for work. As soon as she's gone, I reach for my phone and take a deep, unsettling breath.

There is a heap of new messages from people at school, but I skip past them and open the Facebook app. My palms become sweaty and my hands start to shake. My finger hovers over the photo. My throat becomes dry and my breathing becomes shallow. I can't do this. *Yes, you can. Face up to your mistake.* The voices fight one another trying to take control. I click on the image and start reading the comments.

Sarah Mac - Such a dirty slut.
Lucy Falcon - OMG what a home-wrecker. Go die, bitch!!!
Hannah Holmes - She will get what's coming to her. Her life as she knows it is over.
Dylan Champ - Anyone got her number? I want a taste ;)

The comments go on and on. At least two hundred plus. Everyone in my year knows about it or has commented. I have no one to go to. My phone buzzes in my hand. My chest tightens as I see the name. *Ethan.* I take a moment to click on the message.

Ethan - You tell anyone what happened and I will end you. You wanted it just as much. Everyone knows you threw yourself at me. A photo speaks a thousand words. Thanks for the fun but I don't want you.

I scream out to my empty room and throw my phone across my bed. He's totally right. If I told Mia and my friends what really happened in the locker rooms, they wouldn't believe me. No way I can show up to school tomorrow. I have to get out of here. He's right; my life is over. Everyone at school hates me and will make my days a living hell.

My feet hit the floor and I run into my bathroom before locking the door. It feels like a million knives have stabbed me in the chest. I yank open the bottom drawer of the vanity. I pull everything out of the way until I find what I'm looking for. The sharp edges nip at my skin, but I don't care; I deserve worse. I pull the razor out and turn on my bath. I fall to the ground, wrapping my arms around myself, rocking back and forth until the water is almost overflowing onto the bathroom floor. I don't bother removing my clothes, instead, I jump in. The water engulfs me until everything disappears.

Daring Support

If you too are struggling with what Charlotte has gone through please seek professional help as soon as possible, you don't have to go through this by yourself. There are support systems out there that can listen, support and offer professional advice.
Please refer to page 261 for more information.

Daring Culture: Online Safety

Let's be honest, a lot of our time these days is spent on social media and that's okay, but how do we make it a safe place?

♥ **Remember not everyone online is who they say they are.**
Unfortunately, there are people online who aren't who they pretend to be. People can make fake profiles using someone else's images.

When you talk to someone new, just be wary of them. People can also hack profiles or make public accounts, so never say anything in a DM that you wouldn't say in real life.

♥ **Keep your personal information private, so that people can't use this against you.**
Make sure you don't share personal information, like your address.

♥ **Don't go back to sites where people treat you badly.**
If you have experienced bullying on a website, a Facebook group, or by someone online, don't go back there. Block the person who bullied you and remove yourself from that place.

You have the power to remove yourself from bad situations. Remember, you should always do what's best for your mental health.

♥ **Be careful what you say and make sure you don't offend other people.**
We have all been there—when we say something online that we didn't think would offend someone but it did. The important thing to know is that you should just double-check what you write. If you do unintentionally offend someone, be honest. Tell them that you are sorry and didn't mean it to upset them. Being honest and apologising can make the world of difference.

If You're Cyberbullied

♥ **Think, don't react**
I know it's the first thing we want to do, to reply and stick up for yourself, but honestly, it's not worth it. It's exactly what the bully wants, they want to elicit a response from you.

Instead, ignore and block. You can also report the comment or post to the app you're using. Most social platforms have strict user-codes to protect their customers.

♥ **Tell a trusted adult about it**
Speak to an adult about what has taken place. Get their advice and talk about how it made you feel. Talking about these sorts of things can take the weight off your shoulders.

♥ **Save the evidence**
Screenshot the incident and keep it as evidence that may be used to combat the behaviour in the future.

If people are trying to bring you down to their level, it means that you are above them.

Daring Culture: Cyberbullying

> How to stand up for your friends:

♥ **Stand up**

If you see a friend or even a stranger getting bullied online, stand up for them. Don't go adding fuel to the fire. Instead, tell the bully that it's not cool, and that picking on someone online is not right.

♥ **Support**

Be there for your friend; tell them it's going to be okay. They shouldn't believe what the bully has written. They are better than that.

♥ **Tell a trusted adult about it**

Explain the situation to an adult you trust. They will be able to take this further.

> Not replying is often the smartest thing to do. If you don't engage, the situation is less likely to escalate. You're showing the bully that he or she hasn't won. Charlotte could have spoken up to her mother about them though. She could have reported them and made a stand. Let's make a stand against cyberbullying; let's make it NOT okay.

Think Before You Type

Smile.
Breathe.
Love.

Daring Movement: I am not defined by

Come up with things that don't define you.

- Your body type

Think Before You Type

You are so brave and so strong.

Don't turn your back on yourself.

Suicide check-in

I know there are times in our lives when we think that there's no other way out. We want to end it all for good, to put a stop to it, and to make the pain disappear. Suicide is not the answer.

Don't let the monster take away all your beauty. Be brave and stand tall; you have so much to give this world.

We all have flat days but you know what's brave? Being able to pull through and standing up for yourself.

Keep yourself alive because you have so much to offer the world.

No matter what you've been through you have come out the other side. You have pulled through. You have lived another day because you are brave.

Life has thrown so much at you, but here you are, still here with us, still keeping that head of yours up. You are one in a million, my darling. You are worthy of your life.

A Daring Mantra

Breathe, it's going to be okay. I know your life may seem like it sucks. That it's over, there's no way to stop the pain.

Breathe, you are so brave. You spend each day holding on because you know it's going to be okay.

Breathe, because today is another day, a day full of possibilities. Open those eyes of yours, step outside, and breathe.

Loving yourself is the most beautiful thing you can do.

Daring Movement: Letting The negative go

When negative thoughts take over your mind, you need to find a way to let them out.

Journal prompts

What's bothering me?

How can I get past this?

Why am I feeling like this?

Talk to someone

♥ Speaking our thoughts out loud to a professional or someone we love is so empowering.
♥ We can receive their advice and can develop a more positive mindset.

A love letter to my teenage self
by Madison Schofield

> Madison is an IT Specialist and compassionate empath.

To Madison,

You are so much more than the validation you are looking for in other people. You deserve so much more than cutting pieces of yourself away to fit into a perfect square. You, my **darling**, are watercolour paint spread across rough, porous paper. Seeping into the roots and leaving your mark while maintaining obscurity and **beauty** in the eye of the beholder.

You are stark contrasts of **emotion** and logic, tantalising emerald-green mixed with ocean-deep sapphire. It is more than okay to be contradictory, to be wrong, to be emotional, to have thin skin. It's okay to be mad at the childhood you didn't have. It's normal to grieve the loss of never knowing what a mother's unconditional love is and only experiencing a mother's **love** with strings attached.

Don't look for your worth in other people; look within yourself. You **are so enough**—it is truly unbelievable how enough you are. It's not your fault your mother couldn't love you. She did the best she could with what she knew, as painful as that is to accept. There are pieces of her within you; don't tear apart your skin trying to get her out. Don't grapple with the blood, bones, and tendons within your body in a panic to remove every trace of her. The **Truth** is, she will always be a part of you.

Forgive yourself. You are not perfect. Perfection will not win you love. Just be yourself. You are empathetic, smart, awkwardly funny (embrace it), and fluent in sarcasm. You will find your people who accept you as you are, who love you unconditionally, and those people? They are the chocolate fudge on your already bomb triple-chocolate cake.

It's time to **stop hating yourself**. Nobody is perfect, my sweet girl. Do not miss the collateral beauty in your upbringing. You love so hard; and now? Now it's time to give some of that **love** you offer so freely to yourself.

Love your older self x

I don't trust words.
I trust vibes.

Words are easy to manipulate; vibes can tell you everything.

Trust Issues

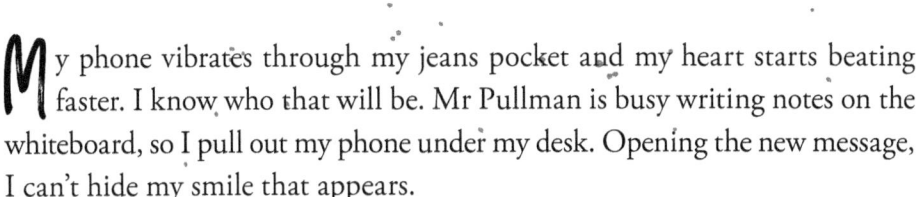

My phone vibrates through my jeans pocket and my heart starts beating faster. I know who that will be. Mr Pullman is busy writing notes on the whiteboard, so I pull out my phone under my desk. Opening the new message, I can't hide my smile that appears.

Liam - Hey, beautiful, I miss you. What u up to?
Me - Just in class listening to the teacher talk shit about algebra.
Liam - I wish I was there with you. We could've had some fun when he wasn't looking ;)

My cheeks heat and Chloe nudges me with her elbow. I glare at her as she points to Mr Pullman, who is looking straight at me. The classroom's attention is right on me. *Oh shit.* I sit up straight and try to hide my phone but it's too late; he's already seen it.

"I will be taking that until the end of class, Ava. See me then." He takes my phone away and part of me dies.

I need my phone so I can talk to Liam.

We have been chatting on Facebook messenger for a few months now. One day, his friend request popped up. We didn't have any friends in common and I nearly didn't accept, but from the moment I saw his profile picture I was done for. I drooled. His bright green and blue eyes stood out against his pitch-black shaggy hair. His profile read:

Name: Liam Price

Age: 18yrs

Location: Melbourne, Victoria

He lives in the same city as me. Well, I live out east of Melbourne but still close enough. He messaged me straight after I accepted his request, asking how I was and then it went from there. We talk every day and went from friends to romance in a matter of weeks. Liam treats me like a princess. He messages me all these nice things. No boy in my school treats me like that.

I've only told Chloe about him. I don't want the whole school or my parents knowing about it—well, until we actually meet in person. We have been sending photos back and forth. We've even done video chats but it's always late at night and I can't see him at all. He's always in the dark.

The bell rings. Thank God today's over. I gather up my books before putting them into my bag.

"I'll meet you at the lockers," Chloe says as she walks past, offering me a smile.

I have to stay back to get my phone from Mr Pullman. He walks towards my desk. *Here comes a lecture in three, two, one …*

"Mobiles are banned from class, Ava. If I see you with this again, it will be detention. Understood?" He passes me my phone and I nod in agreement.

As soon as my phone's in my hands, I sigh in relief. I quickly hurry out of the classroom. As I step into the busy corridor, I check my phone to find five messages from Liam.

Liam – What are you wearing?

Liam – I can imagine you in one of your short school skirts. Your long, toned legs. Your tight school top showing off your perky tits.

Liam – Show me?

Liam – Come on, little kitten.

Liam – Don't be shy.

My cheeks flame as I read through his texts. Someone clicks their fingers in front of my face. I look up to find an irritated Chloe.

"I swear to God, if you ignore me one more time, I'll confiscate your phone and throw it away."

"You wouldn't dare," I say then laugh.

"Oh, but I would. I never get to have girl time with you anymore. Your face is always in your phone." She pouts, slamming her locker door shut.

"I'm sorry. I'll make it up to you."

"So, fill me on with what's happening with Liam? Have you made plans to actually meet him yet?"

I pick up my school bag and we make our way outside through the corridor. "Nah, we haven't met but we have video chatted many times. Maybe I should mention that we need to meet up?"

"Has he shown you his abs?" Chloe asks.

"Ha, it's always dark."

"That's a bit creepy."

"He says he doesn't want to wake his parents," I say then shrug.

"Ah, okay. You need to arrange a meet up. We need to see if he's as perfect as he makes himself out to be." She laughs.

She's right. He seems too good to be true. He's perfect. His effortless looks, his easy-going personality, and best of all, he wants me. No one has ever made me feel so desired before.

We start walking home from school. The sun shines down on us and I close my eyes, lifting my head back. A shiver runs down my spine. I open my eyes, scanning the area.

I find students getting picked up and others walking home like us.

"You feel it again, don't you?" Chloe asks, watching me.

"Yeah, it's weird. I feel like someone is watching us."

"I feel it too. This is getting creepy. It's happening more and more."

We pick up our pace, all while scanning the area looking for anyone suspicious. My phone buzzes as I see some creepy old guy in a dark blue car across the street.

Liam - Did I scare you away?
Me - Sorry. Teacher took my phone away. Just walking home from school. What u doin?

When I look up, the car's gone, disappeared like it was never there. I shake it off.

We walk the short distance to Chloe's house and she hugs me goodbye. Pulling out my phone, I start walking the extra block to my house.

Liam - Just thinking about you.
Me - You're cute. Any plans for the weekend? I was thinking that we should meet up. Would be good to see you in person.

I make it to my house. Just as I turn down my drive, a car drives past and I hear someone wolf whistle. I spin around to see that same blue car from school driving away. I feel sick. That guy was old enough to be my father. *Eww.*

My mother yells hello from the kitchen as I walk past her and straight to my room. I mumble a greeting as I slam my door shut. I can't deal with her today. She would want to know what happened at school and drill me about something annoying. I drop onto my bed and lift my phone out.

Liam - You know that I'm shy.

I roll my eyes as I reply.

Me - Seriously? We're going to go through this again? I want to meet you in person. I've waited long enough. If we want this to go any further, you will meet me this weekend.
Liam - Fine. How about the movies tomorrow? 8pm at Central?

My belly explodes with butterflies. I sit up and quickly dial Chloe's number.

She answers after one ring. "Yo, what's up?"

"Guess what, guess what!?" I scream into the phone.

"Don't tell me, you're pregnant?" she jokes.

"Pfft, as if. Liam is going to meet me at the movie's tomorrow night at Central. Please tell me you have no plans?"

"Eww, I'm not crashing your date."

"No, I want you to come with me, then you can ditch. Maybe ask Christian to come?"

"Why would I ask him?"

"Oh, come on, Chloe, you've been crushing on him for months."

"Fine. I'll get my dad to pick you up tomorrow night."

"You're the best. See ya then."

I hang up and squeal. I can't believe I'm finally meeting him in person.

Liam - As a reward, can you send me something naughty?

My cheeks burn. It's not like we haven't sent naked images to each other, but every time I did it felt weird, like I was doing something wrong. I've never done that with anyone before. But Liam is special.

Me - Only for you ;)

I run to the bathroom and shut the door before locking it. I take a few photos of my boobs for Liam; I pick out the best photo and hit send. His name lights up and he replies instantly.

Liam - Oh yes, you naughty, naughty girl. Send me a photo of you in your school skirt.

I send him more photos as he asked. My stomach churns as I wait for him to reply.

Liam - You're perfect. My naughty little girl, and you're all mine.
Me - :) sure am. Can't wait for tomorrow night.
Liam - Me too.

Saturday drags by painfully slowly. I tell my parents that I'm going to the movies with Chloe. They don't need to know that we are going to meet guys there. They wouldn't let me go if they knew.

At five o'clock, I stand in my room with half my closet thrown across my bed.

I have nothing to wear, as per usual. My wardrobe sucks. I opt for a yellow and white sunflower dress that's tight at the top and flows out at the waist. Liam told me to wear a dress. Slipping the dress over my head, I find a pair of plain flats to match.

I give myself one last look in my full-length mirror. My blond hair is tied up in a ponytail and I have makeup on. But I want to impress Liam. This is going to be the first time we have met in person; I don't want him to be disappointed.

The doorbell rings so I quickly grab my purse from my bed and head for the door. My mother answers, saying hello to Chloe, and she waves to her dad out in the car. I give my mother a kiss on the cheek.

I quickly send a message to Liam.

Me - On my way to Central. You better not chicken out ;)
Liam - Wouldn't dream of disappointing you.

Chloe's dad drops us off out the front of the Central shopping centre. He said he'll meet us back here at ten p.m.

We step inside the mall and it's packed. Late-night shopping is on tonight. I check my phone to see it's five to eight. My stomach explodes with butterflies. I've never been so nervous in my life. I want tonight to go well.

Goose bumps appear over my arms, and Chloe and I both look around.

"I swear to God, someone is watching us again," Chloe whispers. I nod, scanning the area again but I don't see anything suspicious.

She takes hold of my hand and we move towards the escalator before heading down to the cinema. We grab our tickets, some popcorn, Slurpee's,

and sit on the couch near the entrance to the movies. I check my watch; it's right on eight o'clock. Chloe squeezes my arm and I look up to find Christian walking towards us. He leans down before kissing Chloe on the cheek. *Aww, they are too cute.* She gets up and they start talking.

"You guys go in; it'll be starting soon. I won't be long."

"You sure? Don't want us to wait out here with you?" Chloe asks.

"Nah, I'll be fine. Liam won't be too much longer."

Chloe offers me a smile and they head into the theatre. I pull out my phone, about to message Liam, when I see a text from him.

Liam – You look so hot, babe. I'm already in the movies, seat 5B. Meet me here.

I check the time again; it's only five past. Did he walk past us? Why didn't he meet us here? Something doesn't feel right but I brush it off. It must just be my nerves playing with me.

I head into the theatre and manage to find aisle five. It's dark in here with only the lights on the ground. I look up to find Chloe and Christian two rows behind. She gives me the thumbs-up and I wave back. I step into the aisle, keeping my head down, and move towards seat C. I see Liam's shadowy figure and quickly drop into my chair as the movie starts up in the background. *This is it.* I turn to say hello to Liam.

I feel numb, I can't breathe. It's not Liam. It's an old guy with a receding hairline and he's smiling down at me. He reaches out to touch my leg, but I scream and stand up. I turn to run but he grabs on to my arm, stopping me. I scream louder—I'm making a scene. "Let me go. You're in my boyfriend's seat," I yell at him.

He goes to open his mouth but Chloe and Christian pull me free of his grip. We hurry down the aisle.

"I am Liam," he says.

I stop in my tracks. I turn around to look at him again. Then it hits me. He's the guy in the car. The one I saw at school and outside my house. I feel sick. He isn't Liam. This is a misunderstanding.

"Stay away from her, you freak, before I call the cops," Chloe yells at him.

We must have made it outside, but I don't remember a thing. My mind is going a million miles an hour. Who was that guy? Where is Liam? What the hell is going on?

Chloe has her arm around me as we sit on a park bench, waiting for her dad to get us. She called him, saying that we needed to be picked up now. My phone buzzes and my heart beats faster. *Please let this be a mistake. Please.* I open the message.

Liam - Why did you run from me? You're mine, remember?

The phone drops out of my hand, landing on the ground with a thump. Tears fall down my cheeks. How could I have been so bloody stupid? Liam *was* that old creep. Why didn't I see the warning signs? How did I not know?

Daring Support

If you too are struggling with what Ava has gone through please seek professional help as soon as possible, you don't have to go through this by yourself. There are support systems out there that can listen, support and offer professional advice.

Please refer to page 261 for more information.

Trust check-in

Trust. It sounds like an easy thing to do, right? Some of us can trust easily, others not so much. It all depends on how much you have been lied to in the past.

What does it take to trust someone? Is it the time you have spent together? Or is it based on your interests and the friends you have in common?

For me, trust comes from my time spent with a person. Trust has to be earned and that's because in the past, trust has been burnt for me.

When I meet someone, I get a feeling that I can trust them enough to see them again. And then I take it from there. It's an intuition thing.

Sometimes we forget to trust ourselves. We get so caught up with who we are talking to that we push aside our initial thoughts.

The best thing you can do is trust yourself and your instincts.

Do you trust yourself enough to know when you are being lied to? This may be a hard question to answer because our initial response may be to think 'of course, I trust myself'.

I'd like to think that I'd know if I was being lied to, but truthfully, there are people in this world who are very good at manipulation. They have all the right answers. They know how to pull you in until they have you right where they want you. They will say all the correct things until you'll trust them with your own life. You'd do anything for them.

That's how someone could betray you—by pretending to be someone they aren't. By trying to pull you in to earn your trust and then breaking it. Like Liam did with Ava. They built up a relationship online. Liam had all the right answers and for months, built that trust with Ava. But he wasn't who he said he was.

Daring Culture: Who are you, really?

Deep questions you can ask someone if you want to know who they really are:

- What inspires you the most?
- What do you look for in a friend?
- Who has been the biggest influence in your life?
- How would you describe your perfect day?
- How do you recharge?
- What actions help you to trust someone?
- What's your favourite thing to do?
- Do you trust anyone in your life?
- Do you believe in true love?
- What are your biggest fears?
- Who is your hero?
- Who are you when you're alone?
- What's most important to you?

Daring Movement: Share The Love

Take a compliment or pass it on to someone else.

  You are kind

 You are perfect The way you are

 Thank you for being you

 You are enough

 You do you

 Be brave

 Smile

 You are protected

 You are perfect

Daring Culture: Keeping Safe Online

Tips for finding out who you are really talking to online:

♥ **Talk to them over the phone.** This adds another layer of depth to your relationship. From a person's voice, you can often get a sense of their age. Pay attention to how they sound and also the sort of language they use. Is it consistent with yours?

♥ **Video chat.** *Safety reminder:* only do this if you have been talking for a while. You can cover your camera until they come on for safety reasons. That way you can see if they are the same as their photos.

♥ **Ask personal questions.** Get to know them. Ask hard, deep questions.

You, my dear, are as powerful as you believe.

You, my dear, are as powerful as you believe.

Daring Culture: Keeping Safe Online

Tips for finding out who you are really talking to online:

♥ **Talk to them over the phone.** This adds another layer of depth to your relationship. From a person's voice, you can often get a sense of their age. Pay attention to how they sound and also the sort of language they use. Is it consistent with yours?

♥ **Video chat.** *Safety reminder:* only do this if you have been talking for a while. You can cover your camera until they come on for safety reasons. That way you can see if they are the same as their photos.

♥ **Ask personal questions.** Get to know them. Ask hard, deep questions.

Save & Love Yourself First

*D*on't wait around for that person to come into your life who will change everything. This isn't a movie where the guy appears, he tells you that you're beautiful, and you are saved. You need to save yourself first. Otherwise, you will always rely on others to make yourself feel good.

You need to really connect with yourself and know exactly who you are. What you love, what you hate, what your passions are. Don't let someone tell you these things; you need to open up and find out for yourself.

You can't truly love another person until you love yourself first. Give it time.

When I was twenty years old, I realised that in every book I read the girl got saved by a guy. I always questioned why she couldn't save herself? It's not reality.

Once you've saved yourself, then you can fall in love with someone who loves you exactly the way you are, the true you. You will attract your soul mate when you're fully connected to yourself and you may already know it.

This might sound simple, but it can take years. It took me a long time to become my true self and find out who I am. I spent years following the crowd, doing things to be 'cool', doing things that I hated just to fit in. Once you love yourself and know yourself fully, it's the best feeling in the world. You feel as though you're reborn. You connect to yourself like you do no other. You have the ability to give yourself this magical feeling, to feel that connection. To feel loved each and every second of every day.

When you depend on people to lift you up, they'll have the power to bring you down.

You don't need their approval to know your worth.

A love letter to my teenage self
by Amy Molloy

> Amy is a journalist, editor and author for mental health. You can find out more about her here www.amymolloy.com.au

Dear Amy,

Sometimes that forgiveness you crave might be far more subtle than you were hoping for—but it can be just as **healing**. I know that in your heart, you're **hoping** for an apology: for a letter, for a hug, for a do-over, for a fresh start. But that **forgiveness** you want to give—to another person and to yourself—may not be as momentous as you see in the movies. Sometimes it's so gentle that it almost passes you by.

In fact, you will almost give up on forgiveness before it sneaks into your world when you stop **searching** for it. You will spend years trying to 'fix' relationships and force an 'I'm sorry' from another person before it happens all on its own, when you finally let go of the **breath** you've been holding forever.

That argument, those hurtful words, the shame and guilt that you've been carrying for years will not be forgotten but, in union, you will decide to **overcome** them and to let new

You must trust yourself first before you learn to trust another.

love paper over them so you can barely see them anymore.

I know that, right now, you want to talk it out—and fight it out. But there comes a time when talking about a shared history is no longer useful and instead, you will find **peace** in a present that you're creating together in spite of your past.

Neither of you will forget the **moments** that make your **hearts ache,** but time will lessen their sting. And you'll realise you were all doing the best you could with the tools you had at the time.

Forgiving yourself will be hardest of all, but also the most crucial piece of the puzzle. One day, you will let yourself off the naughty step and realise that sometimes you have to go off the rails to get on the right track. You will see your stubbornness, rebelliousness, and even your 'self-servingness' as traits that, today, enable you to be a passionate creator, mother, partner, and daughter.

For now, don't chase **forgiveness** so fiercely. Trust that it will come if you live life with an open palm. Act from a place of love and not fear. Someday, **you will get there.**

Love your older self x

Let's be
who we really are.

Not who the world
wants us to be.

Embrace Our Differences

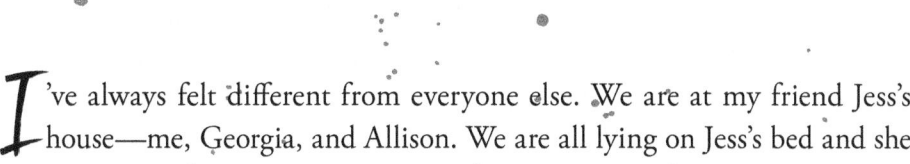

I've always felt different from everyone else. We are at my friend Jess's house—me, Georgia, and Allison. We are all lying on Jess's bed and she goes to get snacks.

"Oh my God, did you see Jackson today?" Georgia squeals, lifting her legs into the air.

Allison laughs, smacking her playfully.

"When are you going to stop gawking and make a move?" Allison teases.

"When I grow some balls."

"Yeah, that's never then," I join in, rolling my eyes.

"What about you, Lil?" Georgia asks.

Allison's eyes find mine. What the hell am I meant to say? I don't find any of the guys in our year or school, for that matter, attractive. Just the thought of touching them makes me almost gag. I can't let the girls know that though; they will think that I'm different.

"Oh, Will's all right I guess." I shrug.

Allison remains quiet but Georgia sits up, facing me.

"You guess? He is frigging adorable. You should so message him," Georgia says, grabbing my phone off the bed.

"No, give it back," I squeal, yanking it from her.

She pokes her tongue out. "You better message him."

"I will," I lie.

Jess comes into the room and throws down packets of chips and lollies on the bed.

"What movie are we going to watch?" Jess asks, picking up the remote to the TV.

She pulls up the Netflix app and we scroll for what feels like hours until she picks a chick flick: *The Duff*. Georgia and Jess lie in front of Allison and me who are leaning against the bedhead. Allison messages her boyfriend, Chris. He's asking what she's doing with us girls. Allison simply replies that we are watching a movie and that they should talk later.

She catches me watching and I blush.

She's so pretty, I wonder what she sees in Chris. She could do so much better; be with someone that treats her like she deserves. Someone like me. As if, *don't be silly*. If I say anything it may ruin our friendship because I know she doesn't feel the same.

My phone buzzes just as the movie starts. Picking it up from next to me, I'm surprised to see a message from Allison.

Allison - This movie is going to suck. Wanna sneak off?

I can't help the smile that finds my lips.

Me - Of course.

Allison jumps off the bed and I follow her to the door.

"Where you two going?" Jess asks, sitting up.

"Just going to get some air. Be back soon," Allison calls over her shoulder as she walks out.

I quickly follow her out. Jess's parents are away for the night, so we have the house to ourselves.

Allison takes my hand; a shiver runs up my arm. It feels so good in mine. She pulls me through the house until we get to the back door. We step outside into the open area. Jess's parents have an undercover deck with couches, a TV, and a firepit.

Allison lets go of my hand and sits on the couch. I join her. The night's silent and my beating heart is the only thing I can hear.

"How are you and Chris going?" I ask, breaking the silence.

I catch her eye roll before she turns to face me.

"Let's not talk about him. I want to talk about you," she says, tucking her beautiful brown hair behind her ear.

"Me? I'm boring; I don't have anyone on the scene anyway."

"I'm glad you don't." She smiles.

My heart starts beating faster and faster. *Is she flirting with me?* Before I get a chance to process it, she leans forward. Her lips are only a centimetre from my own. I stop breathing.

They touch mine and my belly explodes with butterflies. My mouth opens as she deepens the kiss. My eyes close, as her hand wraps around my hair. She pulls at my hair causing a moan to slip from me.

The sliding door bangs open and we both pull away.

"Oh my God," Jess shrieks.

My cheeks flame as I look to Allison, but she doesn't seem to be embarrassed. Georgia is next to Jess with her phone in her hand.

"Did I just imagine that, or did it really happen?" Jess asks, moving towards us.

"Oh, I've got proof that it happened and everyone will know," Georgia says, shaking her phone.

"What the hell are you doing?" Allison growls. She jumps up, trying to grab the phone off Georgia.

Is she really going to put it on social media? This can't be happening. Sweat forms on my forehead.

"It's already done; everyone will have seen it by now." Georgia smirks.

My stomach drops. My phone starts vibrating in my pocket. Lifting it out, I open it to find a heap of messages and comments already. My hand starts to shake as I open Facebook. I click on the photo of Allison and I locking lips. There are more than twenty comments already. I scroll through them and tears well up.

OMG I always knew that Lil was a lezzo.

She loves licking the pussy.

Pussy-lickers.

It goes on and on with hurtful comments. I catch Allison's eye; there is regret written on her face. Like she wants to take it back because now she's

being labelled a lesbian and a cheater. And it's all my fault.

"I can't believe you did that, Georgia. How could you?" Allison yells.

"Not my fault you two were caught locking lips. Your boyfriend deserved to know, and everyone else. It's disgusting. I mean, I already knew that Lil was gay but you? Didn't see that coming," Georgia says. She looks Alison up and down in disgust.

I need to get out of here. Standing, my legs wobble but I manage to push past the girls. I run into Jess's room and grab my bag. Jess meets me at her door, blocking the entrance.

"I'm so sorry, Lil. She shouldn't have done that," she says, lowering her eyes.

I don't reply because I'll just break down. I push past her and run to the front door.

"Lil." Allison is yelling my name, but I can't face her.

My phone starts buzzing in my pocket as I run down the driveway. It keeps ringing and ringing. I stop running once I'm halfway down the street. Lifting my phone out, I see four missed calls; my mother's tried calling twice. I hit her number, and she answers on the first ring.

"Lil, where are you? What's with this image on Facebook?" she asks.

She has no idea that I like girls. What will she think of me now? Will she hate me? Should I be honest with her or tell her it was a big joke? Because it probably was.

"Can you please pick me up? I'm walking down Jess's street." My voice cracks.

"Of course. Be there in a minute."

I hang up before placing my phone back in my pocket. There are a million more notifications, but I can't stand to look at them right now.

Minutes later, Mum comes flying around the corner. She stops next to me and I quickly jump in the car, slamming the door shut behind me. Placing my head in my hands, I let all the tears fall. My mother places her hand on my shoulder, rubbing it back and forth.

"Is it true? Do you like girls?" she asks.

I can't tell her; she won't love me if I do. She will disown me because it's not normal to like the same sex. My parents are Christians and this goes against our religion.

"No, Mum, it was a big joke, but Georgia took it too far," I say, wiping the tears away.

"Oh, I don't want that path in life for you. This isn't going to look good for us." She shakes her head as we drive off. I knew she wouldn't like this. I've ruined our family's reputation, all because of one kiss.

The rest of the drive is spent in silence. We pull up to our driveway and as soon as Mum turns the car off, I'm out of it. My father's in the living room as I pass. One look at him and I know I'm in deep trouble. I try to walk past him, heading straight for my room. I need to be alone.

"Lillian, wait right there," he yells.

My feet stop. I turn around, but I can't meet his eye.

"What is this photo your mother showed me? Don't you know that it's immoral to be with the same sex?" he growls.

"I know, Dad, it was just a joke. It doesn't mean anything." My body starts to shake.

"Go to your room. I don't want to see you again until tomorrow."

I run and shut the door. My body falls against it as I slide to the ground. My phone keeps buzzing. Pulling it out, I see Allison's name on the screen. I find myself answering it.

"Lil, thank you for answering."

I can't form the words to respond so instead I listen.

"I'm so sorry. I don't know what happened tonight, but it can't happen again. Chris is so mad at me. I can't lose him. You know what our parents are like and everyone at school. We need to act like this was just a dare, that it meant nothing. Okay?"

Her words feel like a knife stabbing into my chest. She really regrets it. She doesn't like me like I like her.

I can't reply so I hit the end button. My phone drops from my hand and I lie on the ground. My body's shaking. I'll never be able to be who I truly am. I have to put a mask on, one that covers up who I really am. Why can't this be easy? Why can't I just be and like who I want to?

Daring Support

If you too are struggling with what Lil has gone through please seek professional help as soon as possible, you don't have to go through this by yourself. There are support systems out there that can listen, support and offer professional advice.

Please refer to page 261 for more information.

Be You check-in

Society expects us to act a certain way. But you love who you love, regardless of their sex. Who is anyone to say what's right and wrong? Shouldn't we be able to make our own decisions and follow our own paths?

One thing a good friend once taught me was to 'be who I truly am'.

At the time I didn't understand. I thought, *but I am me, aren't I?*

It wasn't until I actually found myself, found who I am, what I like, and what I don't, that I understood what she meant.

We can spend every day being someone we aren't. Someone who we think we are meant to be. Instead, we should be embracing our true self: dressing how we want to, hanging out with who we want to, and liking who we want to.

If our community doesn't embrace that some of us are different, we need to educate them. Explain that you or your friends are unique, as each one of us should be.

You can't help the way you feel, and you shouldn't have to explain yourself. We should all be educated to accept each person as they are.

If your friend told you that they liked girls, how would you react? Would you turn your back on them and spread around rumours?

OR

Would you smile and say, "that's great" and let her know that she is really brave.

Daring Movement: Love Me

Show yourself some love.
Paste a photo of yourself in the centre of the circle. Around the border, write things that you love about yourself and reminders you want to keep in the forefront of your mind.

Embrace Our Differences

The trick is
as long as you
know who you are
other's opinions
will fade away
into nothing.

Daring Movement: Self check-in

Complete the sentence:

I really like:

I want:

My biggest fear is:

What I love about myself:

Who do I admire and why:

My perfect day is:

Today I'll:

Embrace Our Differences

Be you, for you.

Daring Culture: Standing Up For Yourself

> When Allison called Lil, she said the below:

"I'm so sorry. I don't know what happened tonight, but it can't happen again. Chris is so mad at me. I can't lose him. You know what our parents are like and everyone at school. We need to act like this was just a dare, that it meant nothing. Okay?"

> Lil was hurt. Perhaps, a more daring way to respond would have been something like:

"No, Allison. I'm sorry that we can't be who we are. You initiated things with me because you wanted to. But the moment everyone found out, you took it all back in a heartbeat. That hurts, but I understand it is because you're scared of what everyone's thinking. If you really like me, then drop your mask and let's embrace who we are."

Be you.
Be brave.
Be happy.
Be Thankful.

Daring Movement: Vision Board

Create a vision board.
Paste photos of what you want out of life and love.
Have fun, draw, colour, and write what you desire most.

Own It check-in

We all have our own story to tell, one that shapes us into the women we become. Each day, each situation teaches us a valuable lesson—one we can learn from.

We should never regret anything that we do. Yeah, we will have moments when we mess up so badly that we think our life's over. But you can either sit in your room sulking or you can admit that you stuffed up and learn from it. Take what you've learnt and use it to change.

We aren't made to all be the same. We are made to each be unique. No two people in the world should be exactly the same. We become who we are from life experiences. They shape us to become who we are.

Own who you are, who you like, and what you like.

Daring Culture: You Are In Control

Things you can have control over:

- Your attitude
- Becoming who you want to be
- Embracing your true self
- Who your friends are
- Being who you really are
- Hanging with your people
- Doing what you love
- What books you read
- Your beliefs
- What you love doing
- Who you like and don't like
- Saying no

Embrace Our Differences

Owning your story is the boldest thing you can do.

Daring Movement: Celebrating Uniqueness

Things that make me unique:

My name is:

What makes me different?

My hair colour is:

My eye colour is:

I love playing the:

What can I do that my friends can't?

I'm good at:

My best subject is:

What am I best at in my family?

I love reading books about:

What do I feel called to be?

My favourite TV show is:

On weekends you will find me:

My best feature is:

See how unique you are?

Embrace Our Differences

Own it, flaunt it..

Drop The Mask, Darling

We all wear a mask at one point in our lives. We pretend to like someone just because our friend thinks that they are cool. We reflect a person that we are not. We play dumb because our friend thinks nerds are lame.

What happens when we take off that mask of the person that we aren't? We become who we want to be, someone we are proud of. Someone who does what she wants; someone who isn't scared of shining light on her special talents.

Daring Movement: What A Girl Wants

Ways to find out who you are and what you want.

What or who lights you up?

Who are you when nobody's watching?

If you saw a friend getting bullied, what would you do?

Why are you worth knowing?

What do you want most right now?

What can you offer the world?

How would your best friend describe you?

What would you do if you knew you couldn't fail?

If you could have any superpower, what would it be and why?

Embrace Our Differences

Remove the mask, my darling, you are too brave to hide.

A Love Letter To My Teenage Self
by Julia Clarke

Julia is an author and adventurer at heart.
You can find out more about her here www.authorjuliaclarke.com

Dear Julia,

I've struggled with what to write, not because I don't have enough to say, but rather too much. You are so young, so eager to **explore** the world, so **excited**. And I'm excited for you. There's so much to see and learn, so much you're going to experience. Just don't focus too much on the destination that you forget to **enjoy the journey**.

As you get older, you will see what I mean. How **time** seems to speed up the older you **grow**. How life seems to pass in the blink of an eye. Joy is to be found in the everyday **moments**: the talks you have with Mom on the way to school, the lazy Sundays spent practicing driving with Dad, or watching Legally Blonde together for the millionth time. **Cherish** those moments, those relationships. Because as life goes on, you will get busier.

You will go to college and grad school. You will **focus** on your career and your marriage. And then you will have a child of your own.

I don't want to spoil all the surprises for you—for that's a big part of the fun of life. But I want you to always **remember** to slow down and enjoy. To **be present**. Because life is lived in the moment.

And life is a collection of many **moments** both good and bad. Just remember when the bad ones happen, and they will happen, that there will be good ones too. As one of my favourite football players, Julian Edelman, said (and yes, I'm sure you're shocked to hear that I have a favourite football player, since I'm not really a fan at your age), 'Tough times don't last. Tough people do.' And he's right.

You will face **challenges** you cannot possibly fathom. You will lose friends to cancer and freak accidents. You will experience pain like you've never known. You will be pushed to the brink both mentally and physically, and you will have to claw your way back to life. You will watch loved ones **suffer**. And you will **struggle** with your own shortcomings.

And you know what? You're human. And that's okay. What matters is that you **keep trying**, you keep improving, you

A love letter to my teenage self
by Julia Clarke

> Julia is an author and adventurer at heart.
> You can find out more about her here www.authorjuliaclarke.com

Dear Julia,

I've struggled with what to write, not because I don't have enough to say, but rather too much. You are so young, so eager to **explore** the world, so **excited**. And I'm excited for you. There's so much to see and learn, so much you're going to experience. Just don't focus too much on the destination that you forget to **enjoy the journey**.

As you get older, you will see what I mean. How **time** seems to speed up the older you **grow**. How life seems to pass in the blink of an eye. Joy is to be found in the everyday **moments**: the talks you have with Mom on the way to school, the lazy Sundays spent practicing driving with Dad, or watching Legally Blonde together for the millionth time. **Cherish** those moments, those relationships. Because as life goes on, you will get busier.

You will go to college and grad school. You will **focus** on your career and your marriage. And then you will have a child of your own.

I don't want to spoil all the surprises for you—for that's a big part of the fun of life. But I want you to always **remember** to slow down and enjoy. To **be present**. Because life is lived in the moment.

And life is a collection of many **moments** both good and bad. Just remember when the bad ones happen, and they will happen, that there will be good ones too. As one of my favourite football players, Julian Edelman, said (and yes, I'm sure you're shocked to hear that I have a favourite football player, since I'm not really a fan at your age), 'Tough times don't last. Tough people do.' And he's right.

You will face **challenges** you cannot possibly fathom. You will lose friends to cancer and freak accidents. You will experience pain like you've never known. You will be pushed to the brink both mentally and physically, and you will have to claw your way back to life. You will watch loved ones **suffer**. And you will **struggle** with your own shortcomings.

And you know what? You're human. And that's okay. What matters is that you **keep trying**, you keep improving, you keep doing your best every single day. Some days, it won't seem like enough. But eventually, you'll see that every little bit counts. All those habits, all that self-discipline, all that hard work pays off.

And you'll come to realise that it doesn't really matter if the laundry was done or the bed was made. What matters is that you spent that extra ten minutes with your daughter, pretending to be her favourite puppet. What matters is that you took the time to stop and listen to your mom's concerns. Her fears, her hopes, and her challenges. What matters is that you took a moment to appreciate a *beautiful* sunset or an incredibly moving performance by a talented organist. What matters is that you stopped to *appreciate* the life you've been given, the *blessings* you have.

You may not always like the challenges set in your path, but they will make you *stronger*. They will make you wiser. And I hope that instead of living in fear, you will embrace the unknown, you will *enjoy the journey*.

Lots of love and hugs, *your future self* x

How we start our day sets our mood for the day.

Picture Perfect Vs Reality

Daring Support

If you too are struggling with what Adele has gone through please seek professional help as soon as possible, you don't have to go through this by yourself. There are support systems out there that can listen, support and offer professional advice.
Please refer to page 261 for more information.

The morning light shines in through my bedroom window. My eyes flitter open. The first thing I do is reach for my phone. I open my Instagram and look at all the beautifully styled photos. I see what people eat, what they are wearing, places they've visited, and who they've hung out with.

One photo catches my attention; it's a chick from my school. A popular girl. She's in her bed, looking like she just woke up. She looks perfect: her skin is flawless, her hair is in a perfected high bun, nothing out of place. I try to smooth down my bed hair, but it's no use.

Pushing back the sheets with my feet, I walk over to the mirror. My reflection is nothing like hers.

Where her hair is perfectly styled, mine is everywhere. I've got a mullet hanging out the bottom with a rat's nest on top of my head.

Looking into my own eyes, I feel the judgment, the hatred for myself. *Why don't I look like her?* Looking farther down, I notice the scars that line my cheekbones and chin. Pimples are scattered all over my face, along with freckles on my nose, nothing like her perfect, flawless skin. A solitary tear falls effortlessly down my cheeks.

"Why can't I be like her?" I whisper at myself in the mirror.

I'll never be able to get anyone, looking like this. I'll never be able to be anyone special.

Picture Perfect Vs Reality

May you always have the courage to chase your dreams.

Morning Routine check-in

Our day starts off with the first thing we do in the morning. We set up our day with our first action. Picking up your phone is the first thing that you want to do, to check your social media accounts and see what you've missed, but this isn't the healthiest way to wake up. If you see something that makes you upset or angry, you will take this into your day, even subconsciously. If we were to change that one little habit and instead do something you love first thing, you will go into your day with a positive attitude.

Journaling is a great way to start the day. You can let go of things from yesterday so you're not carrying those with you. You can set your mood, your intentions, and your goals.

Other suggestions to try; meditating to let things go and move forward with positive energy, reading a book to escape into another world and morning affirmations to give yourself all that self-love you deserve.

Daring Movement: Morning Journal

Something I'm letting go of from yesterday …

Today I'm looking forward to …

Today I'll feel …

Today I'm grateful for …

You are in charge of how you feel. Be kind to yourself.

Meditation

Meditation is a great way to start your day. You can download an app on your phone that has a choice of meditation soundtracks. These are great because you can put in your headphones and be talked through a meditation. When we hear the word 'meditation' it may sound scary, maybe something that you have to be skilled to do but that isn't the case. With a guided meditation, you don't have to do anything apart from listen to the instructor and do as they say. They can give you great tips to take into your day, and when you are feeling overwhelmed, you can practice your breathing and get back into the right headspace.

Daring Culture: How To Meditate

Guided apps for mediation:

- ♥ Insight Timer
- ♥ Headspace
- ♥ Calm
- ♥ Stop, Breathe & Think
- ♥ The Mindfulness App

Daring Movement: Daily heart check-in Meditation

Place your hand over your heart, take a big deep breath, hold, and exhale. Feel the beating of your heart. Breathe into your heart and tell it something you love about yourself. Now let it out and smile.

Breathe in again and ask your heart what it needs. What is it missing at this moment? Release your breath and say thank you. You may not get your answers straightaway but be aware of little hints throughout the day.

Daring Culture: Morning Affirmations

> Thirty morning affirmations to say out loud while looking in the mirror:

I am ...
- Beautiful
- Courageous
- Mindful
- Powerful
- Kind
- Confident
- Creative
- Compassionate
- Determined
- Daring

Today I'll ...
- Feel empowered
- Believe in myself
- Be humble
- Overcome a fear
- Make someone feel special
- Treat myself with kindness
- Be grateful
- Shine brightly
- Be aware of my needs
- Do something brave

My life is ...
- What I make it
- Full of love
- A blessing
- Empowering
- Inspirational
- Full of possibilities
- Limitless
- Worthwhile
- Shining bright
- Evolving

Affirmation deck by Shining Your Light

A filter puts a mask on you, one that covers your true beauty.

Daring Movement: Today's Plan

I woke up at: M   T   W   T   F   S   S

Mood as a symbol:

I feel:

Three priorities for today:

1.

2.

3.

Today's quote:

The Real You check-in

We upload our lives to our social media feeds. We upload what we are doing, who we are with, how much fun we're having, and all that awesome sparkling stuff, but what about our struggles? Do you post when you're having a bad day? We see these influencers and their feeds are full of them living the high life. They're flooded with made-up faces, reppin' products, and going out for long lunches.

Why can't we be real? We all have down days. Let's share our struggles, our makeup-free faces, and what we are actually going through. Most of us can't afford to go out for every meal. Some of us are going through struggles at home. Many of us feel so worthless that we feel like we aren't living life the right way. Because not much can live up to the influencer-created expectations. We are all unique and each live a different life; let's be real.

Picture Perfect Vs Reality

Embrace your flaws. They make you who you are, inside and out.

Daring Movement: Me In A Jar

Fill this jar with everything that makes you, you. Your traits, your flaws, and everything that makes you unique. Add little notes, pictures anything that represents you.

Picture Perfect Vs Reality

Step away from the fake world and into the real one.

Social Media check-in

It's so tempting to grab your phone when you are bored or waiting for someone. But have you ever had a day off social media?

I now have a rule that's called Switch-off Sunday. Honestly, it took me a few weeks to make this a habit but now it's something that comes naturally. When Sunday rolls around, I know it's a day off social media—a day dedicated to me and my needs. I was surprised at how present I became in situations. I got more done and accomplished things that I kept putting off. Like me, you may find a new hobby or a new friend by getting out there in person.

We have made it the social norm that when you are by yourself or waiting for something, you go to your phone. But if you resist this urge, it becomes easier and easier to be more present in a situation. Try the 'Switch-Off Sunday' rule, you'll feel refreshed and ready to start your week off on a good note.

Daring Movement: Ritual Days

My weekly routine days.
Let's set up some ritual days that you can focus on each week.

Example: Fitness Mondays, Creative Tuesdays, Go-to-bed-early Wednesdays, etc.

Monday	
Tuesday	
Wednesday	
Thursday	
Friday	
Saturday	
Sunday	

Picture Perfect Vs Reality

A love letter to my teenage self
by Amanda Rootsey

> Amanda is an author, youth mentor, and life coach. You can find out more about her here www.amandarootsey.com.au

Hey Mandy,

I just wanted to let you know that you're doing okay. It's been a tough year and you feel like your world has been turned on its axis. Mum and Dad splitting up is **not your fault,** and it feels like there should be something you can do about it, but you can't. Just keep doing your thing. And on that, don't be afraid to share how you're feeling. It will feel uncomfortable at first but it's such an important part of rebuilding your relationships. You can do it. It's okay to let Dad know how annoyed you are at him!

Trust your instincts ... actually, you know what? Start by just tuning in and **listening.** Take note of that feeling in the pit of your stomach—it never lies.

You can do anything in this life, but mostly, what I'd love for you to do is realise **you are strong.** So strong. And it's okay to say 'no' sometimes. It's more than okay. You're a kind, gentle soul—don't try to be anything else. Forget what everyone is doing and who you think everyone wants you to be. You're **perfect** just as you are.

The only trouble you've ever gotten into, the only things that might make you feel a little bit crap in life, only come up when you do things you aren't one hundred percent committed to. Don't bother if you don't really want to do something. Only then will you start to **live** from your **heart** and will you honestly be MORE giving and kind because you'll do it **sincerely**. A kind gesture for the wrong reason or without sincerity is not kind at all.

And **please, please, please** take care of yourself. Be gentle with yourself. You, my darling, are a bit of an introvert. All that means is that you do actually enjoy your own company (or you will, once you realise that you can actually be in a room on your own without music blaring!). That's okay. Not everyone is supposed to be loud and the life of the party—**just be you.**

Oh, and keep those flanno shirts and your Docs—that '90s grunge trend is totally coming back. 90210 will never be cool. Hansen are a one-hit wonder, just so you know. Oh, and Take That ... keep your eyes on Robbie—the rest don't do much.

Over the next fifteen years or so, you will find the most **incredible** man to share your life with (not the loser who threatens to burn down Mum's house ... not a good choice!). You will model around Australia and through Europe. You will get a uni degree. You will start your own business. You will beat stage-four cancer. But please **don't be afraid**. You are stronger than you think and you will get through it by tuning into that heart of yours and **Trusting yourself**.

Life will take you on the most magnificent journey and you will find a spiritual teacher, go vegan, and realise just how important it is to take care of your body and make the most of every single moment. It will take **patience**. It will push you. But it will put things into **perspective** in a way nothing else can.

Just keep going with the flow, trying different things, and **following your curiosity**. Oh, and one last thing: don't let those beautiful friendships you have at school fade away ... You've got some really beautiful, kind girls in your life, even if you go in different directions for a while. Cherish them and your beautiful fam.

I love you.
Mandy Moo (some people who love you call you that now—ha!) from the future xxx

Stand Up

Once you learn to **love** yourself fully, every single thing about you, you will **shine** brightly and nothing anyone says or thinks about you will **matter.**

You are a **beautiful**, unique human being who will shine your **light** to the whole wide world.

The bell rings. *Lunchtime, thank God.* I couldn't stand listening to the teacher for another second. Everything she's said for the past thirty minutes has gone through one ear and out the other. I couldn't concentrate, and I had to look cool in front of my friends. We don't like to listen to the teacher. Instead, we wrote notes to each other, complaining or talking about someone in the room. I like writing notes but when we talk about someone else, picking on them, it doesn't sit right with me. But I can't say that to my friends; they would hate me. I would be kicked out of their group, for real.

Tess, Rachael, and Monica walk out of the classroom and I follow them out. We collect our lunch from our lockers and head onto the oval before sitting in our usual spot right near the canteen. We settle in, eating our lunch. I nibble on my sandwich, noticing Monica hasn't touched hers. She grabs her sandwich, takes it to the bin, and throws it out. *Isn't she hungry?* She hasn't eaten all day. I thought she would be starving by now.

I consider my own sandwich, instantly feeling guilty for taking a bite. Did she skip hers to lose weight? Should I be doing the same? I feel sick thinking about throwing out food that my mother bought and made for me. It is such a waste. But if Monica is doing it, should I start?

"Hey, have you seen Brittany lately? OMG, she is so fat," Tess says.

I follow her line of sight and Brittany is right in front of our group. Brittany's face falls and she runs straight for the toilets.

I feel so bad for her. How do we know what she's going through?

I laugh along with the other girls, afraid to speak up for Brittany.

Not Monica, though. She doesn't laugh. She doesn't speak. She just places her hand over her stomach, like she's trying to flatten it. She isn't even fat, not in the slightest. If she thinks she's fat, then I must be too.

Putting down my lunch, I look to Tess. She's not eating. So, I do the one thing that my mother would kill me for; I walk over to the bin and throw out my sandwich. Glancing back over my shoulder, I catch Tess's eye; she nods in approval.

My stomach instantly drops. I was right. I'm overweight.

Daring Support

If you too are struggling with what Jasmine has gone through please seek professional help as soon as possible, you don't have to go through this by yourself. There are support systems out there that can listen, support and offer professional advice.

Please refer to page 261 for more information.

Use Your Voice check-in

Too often we don't speak up for good. We sit there playing words out over and over again in our head. We wonder if we did say what we really wanted to, what would people think of us? Would we get laughed at or told off? Let's stand up for what we believe in. Because it will help change the world for the better.

Daring Culture: It's Not Okay

"Hey, have you seen Brittany lately? OMG, she is so fat," Tess says.

I follow her line of sight and Brittany is right in front of our group. Brittany's face falls and she runs straight for the toilets.

I feel so bad for her. How do we know what she's going through?

I laugh along with the other girls, afraid to speak up for Brittany.

> Jasmine should have used her voice here. She was already thinking about how bad it was for Tess to say that. If she had stood up for Brittany, things could have gone differently.

"Hey, have you seen Brittany lately? OMG, she is so fat," Tess says.

I follow her line of sight and Brittany is right in front of our group. Brittany's face falls and she runs straight for the toilets.

I feel so bad for her. How do we know what she's going through?

I turn around, facing the girls. "That's not a nice thing to say, Tess. You don't know what she's going through. We are all built differently."

Using your voice is the bravest thing you can do.

Use it to stand up for others who might not know how to.

Daring Movement: Using Your Voice

It's time for you to use your voice.
Reply to these comments and practise standing up for your friends:

"Oh my God, she's so fat."

"I heard that she has to see a therapist."

"No wonder Justin broke up with her; she's so pathetic."

"Did you see her hair this morning? Gross."

People are going to talk no matter what you do.

So, do whatever the hell you want.

Daring Movement: My Body

Write and colour in this outline of your body
with what you want to feel from now on.

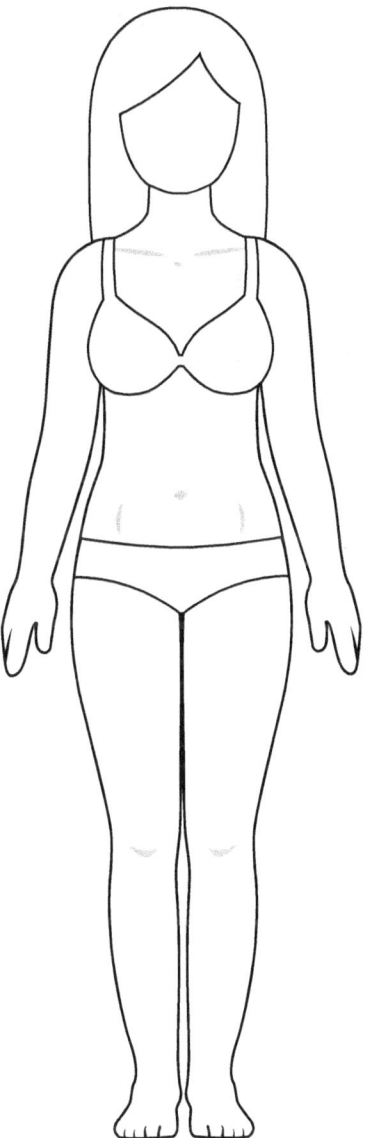

Example: add a big smile if you want to feel happy.

Stand Up 237

A love letter to my teenage self
by Danielle Burrows

> Danielle is a writer who creates from the heart, while inspiring others to do the same. Watch out for her upcoming affirmation deck at www.fromwallflowertowildflower.com

To the me I once was,

First up, hi. I see you. I see your **hopes** and **dreams**—those out-of-this-world, bigger-than-you-can-imagine dreams.

I *feel* you, too. The way your **heart** hurts—that big heart, overflowing with emotion, angst, and care. I get it. Sometimes it feels too big for you to carry. But you can and you do.

How you feel now isn't how you'll always feel. You remember that and *you'll be okay*.

Let me start by saying this: not everything is going to go according to plan. But before you let your heart break, also hear me when I say ... that's a good thing! Because sometimes our plans don't fit into the **bigger picture**. And that bigger picture? Girl, it's something to behold.

So, don't stress about your goals. Do the work, sure, **fight** with all your heart to make them a reality, but also *enjoy* the moments leading up to them. Because once you reach them, the goalposts move, and the journey starts again. Don't let that journey become a battle. The moment you put pressure on your dreams to give you something, the less joy you'll feel doing it. So enjoy it. Bring yourself back to the reason why you chose that path to begin with. I can guarantee it always starts from a **place of joy.**

Hot tip: You don't have to marry the first guy you fall for. It's okay to have some fun and **break some hearts.**

I know you won't, though. Because you're careful. Such a good girl. Your head is clear and you've got yourself figured out. You like to make your own mind up and go your own pace. There is NOTHING wrong with that. Don't let anyone tell you otherwise. If people don't know you, then their opinion isn't valid.

At all times, you are exactly where you need to be.

It's so important to understand that you don't need to compare yourself to anyone else. Sometimes, I know you feel judged or **misunderstood,** as if people take one look at you and conclude something that is way off the mark. I need you to realise that you are fine the way you are. Some might say beautiful. Know your heart and truth. Believe it. Own it. Who wants to be the same as everyone else anyway?

Embrace your difference. Stay true to yourself. Here's another spicy tip: if you are yourself, fully and completely, then you'll only ever attract people who fit.

In a way, I'm glad time travel doesn't exist and you won't read this letter. Because if you did, something might shift and change, and we'd end up somewhere completely different than where we are right now.

Secret: I'm happy. You're **happy**.

Also ... you will fall in love. And that love will grow. I remember the moment you were afraid that no one would ever love you. It happens and it feels great.

You'll have children, too.

And you'll find your **passion**. Not the one you have now—a new one. Then another one after that. I'm telling you, life is **rewarding**. You can be whatever the hell you want to be. And you've got the determination to do it.

Trust that. ***Trust yourself.***

Love,
The one you are now

Blame Game

It's okay to fall out of love with someone. We all change throughout our lives— we outgrow some people we used to hold so close.

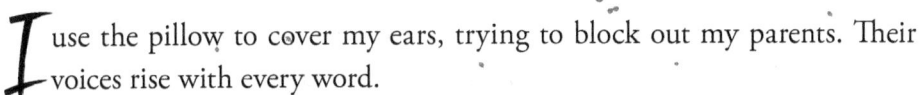

I use the pillow to cover my ears, trying to block out my parents. Their voices rise with every word.

"What about the fucking kids?" my father screams.

"We should never have had them. We were never right for each other," my mother yells.

A piercing slap of skin against skin has me sitting upright in bed. My mother cries out. *What was that?*

I push back the sheets and run to my door. Opening it slightly, I peer out to find my parents in the hallway. My mother has tears rolling down her face, her hand on her cheek. My father stands completely still.

"I'm so sorry. I didn't mean to do that," he says, then covers his face in his hands.

"We need to tell the kids. It's time." My mother wipes away a tear.

I step out into the hallway. "Tell us what?"

Time seems to stop; my parents stay silent. *What were they fighting about now?*

"I'm sorry, Kate, but we have decided it's best if I go away for a while," my father says quietly.

All the air from my lungs disappears. "Go where? Why?"

My father takes a step forward as I take one back. *Please don't say it. Don't say it.*

"Your mother and I haven't been getting on the past few months, as you've probably noticed. We don't want to fight in front of you anymore, so we think it's best if I go stay somewhere else for now."

"Have I done something?" I ask.

"Of course not, sweetie. This has nothing to do with you. It's between your father and me." My mother tries to pull me in for a hug but I take a step back. This is all too much. I don't want him to leave.

I can't stand being here another second. I need air. I turn on my heel and run. Straight down the hall, out the front door, and I don't stop.

"Kate, come back here," my mother screams down the road.

But I don't look back. I keep running until I'm out of breath. I run until my legs give out and I fall to the ground. The gravel scrapes against my knees but I let the pain in. My face falls into my hands and tears soak my cheeks.

I stay on the footpath, leaning against someone's front fence until the sun starts falling beneath the trees. Then I start walking back home, wondering what I'll walk into. Will my father already be gone? Will I ever see him again? Can I go with him? They said it wasn't my fault, but what if there was something more I could have done? I could have tried harder at school, or not gone to that party. Maybe it wasn't me overall—but those little things. What about Christmas and birthdays? Will we have to choose between them? What if they see other people? I feel sick.

I push open the front gate to find the front door wide open. I step inside to find bags packed next to the door. My heart starts beating faster. My father walks down the hallway before throwing another bag on the pile. I stand there frozen in place. He stops in front of me, pulling me in for a hug. I wrap my arms around him, never wanting to let go, afraid that when I do, he'll be going.

"This isn't goodbye, Kate. We will work this out. Okay?" He pulls back and I nod, even though I don't believe him. I have a feeling that he won't be coming back to live here.

My little sister appears next to me and I take her hand in mine. She's too young to know what's going on but one day she will realise this is the moment that our family broke apart and there wasn't anything we could do about it.

Daring Support

If you too are struggling with what Kate has gone through please seek professional help as soon as possible, you don't have to go through this by yourself. There are support systems out there that can listen, support and offer professional advice.
Please refer to page 261 for more information.

Blame Game check-in

You should never feel like you are at fault for someone else's decision. Sometimes those we love make decisions that we wish they hadn't, but at the end of the day, they are doing what's best for them. In a perfect world, we would love for our parents to stay together forever. But sometimes it's not possible.

Everything happens for a reason. Odds are, the person you like now probably won't be the same in five years. We change as we grow and that's okay.

Daring Culture: 10 Things I Can and Can't Control

I can control:

- How often I smile
- How I act
- Using my voice
- Setting my boundaries
- How I respond to challenges

I can't control:

- How others act
- What others say
- Decisions people make
- What people think
- What happens between others

Daring Movement: My Dreamiest Day

> **My dreamiest day.**
> Write down how you would live your best day from start to finish.
> What would you do? Who would you hang with?
> There are endless possibilities.

_____
_____
_____
_____
_____
_____
_____
_____
_____
_____
_____

Daring Movement: Daily check-in

What happened today?
_____
_____
_____

What was a highlight from today?

What didn't I like about today?

One word to sum up my day is:

Blame Game

Change could be the start of something great.

A love letter to my teenage self
by Lauren Clarke

> Lauren Clarke is an award-winning editor of fact and fiction. You can find out more about her services at http://www.CREATINGink.com

Hey, younger me,

I have a secret. It's pretty big, so get ready. This is literally all you need to survive the next twenty or so years of your life.

You.

That's it. The one single thing.

Right now, you feel like a pinball whizzing around the machine, flipping from one intense, all-encompassing emotion to the next. You cry **happy** tears, you cry **sad** tears, and you cry **everything** tears ... but you're going to **be okay**.

You'll use tools to cope. Tools therapists gave you, and tools you found yourself. You'll write, you'll meditate, you'll talk, you'll run, you'll sing, you'll dance, and you'll love—**oh, how you'll love**.

You'll follow the **rules** and you'll learn that actually, you kind of love rules. You'll make **mistakes,** but they'll be ones that make you **stronger**, faster, smarter. In fact, in your entire life to date, there's only one thing you actually regret—just one thing. And you're even starting to forgive yourself for that.

I don't want to tell you to be **kinder** to your body (but seriously, the "fat" you think you are now is actually pretty hot). I don't want to tell you to not date this guy or that guy, because they were part of the journey you went through to find your happily ever after. I'm not here to lecture you.

All I want is for you to **be you**. To love. To **be kind**. And to know that actually, you already have everything you need. You're going to be fine.

Love from,
Your older self

PS: Don't do drugs.

Teenage Boys

Although we've heavily featured girls throughout this book, all people of all genders go through these issues and we hope this book will support all teens, regardless of gender, sexuality or identity.

Body image

Just like girls, boys go through body image struggles. When we hit puberty, our body changes. We all go through this at different times and ages. With males, their voices change and they have to get to know their new bodies as they transform into adults. They may have big mood swings just like girls do.

Peer pressure / Putting on a mask

Being a teenage boy isn't easy. You have to grow up quickly and fit in with the 'it' crowd. Peer pressure is a big issue because you have to do things to fit in, things that you may not agree with or want to do. You have to pretend to be someone you may not be just because you don't want to be on the outer. The mask that you put on covers up the boy you once were.

Teenage Boys

We are all going through something.

Treat everyone around you with nothing but *kindness.*

Suicide

This can be a big issue for boys and men because they tend to bottle everything up. Toxic masculine culture deems it weak to talk about your feelings. So, boys will often bottle them all up until it gets to be too much. We need to ask our brothers, friends, and family members if they are okay. Try to be there for them. Let them know that you are there to listen to them.

Depression

Not expressing feelings can cause you to keep them all hidden inside, which can lead to severe depression. You may not want to leave your house for fear of what people will think of you. It can be too hard to get out of bed, too hard to pretend to be okay.

If you see a loved one in this situation, be there for them. Talk to them, ask them to play a game with you, and try to get them moving. Tell them how much you love them and what you love about them. In the moment, you may think it won't help but trust me, with each little compliment offered, you are giving them hope.

Dear reader,

    I see you sitting there, alone in your room. I see the **smile** that plays on your lips, and the **hope** that sparkles in your eyes. The ***daring journey*** you are on isn't easy, but you are making it through. You will keep on keeping on. You are **strong, fierce,** and one of the most daring people in existence.

    You opened to the first page, and your stomach felt warm with **inspiration**.

    With each page read, the dread slowly lifted off your shoulders. You've unearthed **strength** you didn't realise you had, and you've built a resolve to be **True** to yourself.

    As you turn the final page of this book, I'd love for you to make a **promise** to yourself to **be True** to who you are, do what you love.

    May Daring Journey continue to guide you and be there for you when you need it the most.

With **love,**

Jenna Lee

About The Author

I'm Jenna,

USA Today Bestselling Author, Creator and Mentor. Most days you can find me writing out the stories that take over my mind, supporting my friends, creating or designing.

I am mostly known for being a go-getter, a book worm and passionate human who loves nature, all things creative and using my experience to empower other aspiring writers and creatives to bring their light to the world.

Through my own personal journey of overcoming bullying and self-discovery to go on to become a published author and successful business owner. I aim to be an example to inspire other writers, creatives and young people to be who they want to be because I believe they can be anything they want if they put their minds to it.

I remember doing things I regretted just to be cool, following the crowd just to fit in and not feeling strong enough to say no and go my own way but it got to a point when I knew I couldn't keep living like this and I had a little voice inside that told me I was made for bigger and better things. That I would help shape the world in some way.

At the age of 20 (6 years ago) I started my own successful small business 'Jlee' making screen printed homewares and accessories and wrote my very first book that went on to become #1 Bestseller on Amazon in its first week of release.

The writing industry isn't for the faint hearted. I have learned a lot after releasing my first book and even though I sometimes still let the negative self talk in I am learning to focus on the positive, do what I love and giving it my all and my mission is to support you to be true to yourself, write what you love and confidently sharing that with the world.

With love, Jenna Lee

Keep The Daring Journey going

Follow Jenna online
www.jennalee.biz/daringjourney
www.instagram.com/daringjourney

Workshops and Coaching
Jenna is a qualified Youth Mentor you can find out more about her workshops and coaching here
www.jennalee.biz

Contact
Jenna@jennalee.biz

Daring Support

Online support:

www.youthbeyondblue.com
www.thebutterflyfoundation.org.au
www.headspace.org.au/eheadspace
www.biteback.org.au
www.copmi.net.au/kids-young-people
www.au.reachout.com
www.whatworks4u.org
www.suicidecallbackservice.org.au/

Over The phone support:

Beyond Blue: 1300 22 4636
Butterfly Foundation (Foundation for Eating Disorders): 1800 33 4673
Kids Helpline: 1800 55 1800
Suicide Call Back Service: 1300 659 467
Lifeline: 13 11 14
Headspace: 1800 650 890

In person support:

Headspace have centres across Australia.
www.headspace.org.au

Recommended Resources

Books

Shine From Within: A Teen Girl's Guide to Life by Amanda Rootsey
The Anxiety Survival Guide for Teens by Jennifer Shannon
You Don't Have to Learn Everything the Hard way by Aunt Laya Saul

Apps

Insight Timer – Mediation
Smiling Mind
Rise Up + Recover
MindShift
Mindful Gnats

Support

www.about.au.reachout.com
www.thebutterflyfoundation.org.au
www. futuredreamers.com.au
www.youthbeyondblue.com

Podcasts

411 Teen
Youth Mentor Podcast
TED Talks
Youth Radio

Thank You

This book wouldn't be possible without the support of all these people. I have wanted to write this for years, but I've never had the courage or confidence to complete it. This book isn't just for helping others it's been a healing experience for myself as well. Some of the stories have come from my own experiences and others around me. Writing them out has been a massive healing experience for me, one that has helped me let go. Writing is my therapy, a way to let go and put myself into characters, to share stories of real-life events that people go through.

Mum and Dad – Thank you for always believing in me, you've never said that I couldn't do something. You've always given me strength that I can be and do whatever my heart desires. I may have pushed you away during my teenage years but you both never gave up on me. You were always there offering advice even if I didn't want to hear it at the time. Thank you for sticking with me through my darkest and best days.

Dillon – You have always encouraged me and given me the confidence that I always needed. I've always looked up to you as a role model, you are who you are, and you don't change for anybody. That's what I admire most about you. We've been through so much together and I'm so grateful to have you in my life. Thank you for being the best housewife while I worked on this project, you're the best!

Shannon – My bestie, the one that has always encouraged me and been my number one supporter. You've always bragged about me to all your friends, family, and even strangers! Telling anybody that will listen how amazing you think I am. I adore you, you're the most kindhearted, honest, and bestest friend I've ever had. I value your opinion above anybody else's because I know it's going to be the truth no matter what. Thank you for always being there for me.

Lauren – You came into my life at the perfect time, you've helped bring *Daring Journey* to life. You've pushed me, encouraged and made this happen. They say your mentors are people that you look up to and aspire to be and you so are. You're not only my mentor and editor but you're a dear friend to me. Thank you from the bottom of my heart for your support, input, and for just being there for me. Keep smiling beautiful lady because we need more people like you in the world.

Amanda – They say that people come into your life for a reason and, Amanda, I have to admit you have changed my life. I remember when we chatted about *Daring Journey* back at the very beginning, when I didn't have a name for it just little ideas of what I wanted it to be like. Together we brought it to life, our endless chats about the structure, the name and turning it into not only a book but a business too. You are so kind, so gentle and such an inspiring lady. Mentors play such a huge role in people's life's and I'm so lucky to have found you at the perfect time because Daring Journey wouldn't have happened if I didn't. Keep on shining, beautiful, and changing people's lives.

To you the reader – Thank you for taking the time to read *Daring Journey*. I hope that you've enjoyed our journey together and I want you to know that it doesn't end here. I believe in you and know that you are going to live an amazing life and be the most confident, beautiful person. I'm always here for you if you need.

www.ingramcontent.com/pod-product-compliance
Lightning Source LLC
Chambersburg PA
CBHW072339300426
44109CB00044B/2039